COUNTRY HARDBALL

STEVE WEDDLE

TYRUS
BOOKS

F+W Media, Inc.

Published by
TYRUS BOOKS, an imprint of F+W Media, Inc.
10151 Carver Road, Suite 200
Blue Ash, OH 45242. U.S.A.
www.tyrusbooks.com

"The Ravine" previously published in *Crime Factory*, edited by Keith Rawson, Cameron Ashley, and Jimmy Callaway, copyright © 2011 by New Pulp Press, ISBN 10: 0-9828-4364-X, ISBN 13: 978-0-9828-4364-2.
"This Too Shall Pass" previously published in *Protectors*, edited by Thomas Pluck, copyright © 2012 by CreateSpace Independent Publishing Platform, ISBN 10: 1-4792-3647-0, ISBN 13: 978-1-4792-3647-3.
"That Kind of Face" previously published in *Collateral Damage*, by DoSomeDamage .com, copyright © 2011 by Needle Publishing, ASIN: B0055HFTG8.
"Smoke Fades Away" previously published in *D*CKED*, edited by Greg Bardsley, Kieran Shea, Jedidiah Ayres, copyright © 2011 by D*CKED Industries, ASIN: B005IQZQ8W.
"How Many Holes" previously published in *Off the Record*, edited by Luca Veste, copyright © 2011 by Guilty Conscience Publishing, ISBN 10: 1-4709-7585-8, ISBN 13: 978-1-4709-7585-2.

Hardcover ISBN 10: 1-4405-7080-9
Hardcover ISBN 13: 978-1-4405-7080-3
Trade Paperback ISBN 10: 1-4405-7081-7
Trade Paperback ISBN 13: 978-1-4405-7081-0
eISBN 10: 1-4405-7109-0
eISBN 13: 978-1-4405-7109-1

Printed in the United States of America.

10 9 8 7 6 5 4 3 2 1

This is a work of fiction. Names, characters, corporations, institutions, organizations, events, or locales in this novel are either the product of the author's imagination or, if real, used fictitiously. The resemblance of any character to actual persons (living or dead) is entirely coincidental.

Many of the designations used by manufacturers and sellers to distinguish their product are claimed as trademarks. Where those designations appear in this book and F+W Media was aware of a trademark claim, the designations have been printed with initial capital letters.

Cover images ©123rf.com/manfredxy/Patricia Hofmeester/mihtiander.

This book is available at quantity discounts for bulk purchases.
For information, please call 1-800-289-0963.

For Helen

Acknowledgments

Thanks to my agent, Stacia Decker of the Donald Maass Literary Agency, for her faith and generosity and for finding a great home for this book.

Thanks to Ben LeRoy and Ashley Myers and everyone at Tyrus Books for making these stories a book.

Thanks to my parents for lining the walls with books and for requiring my attendance at all those family reunions, church homecomings, and hospital visits across the south.

Thanks to the dedicated handful of people who continue to read my early morning e-mails and respond with notes and thoughts about the four or five attached pages, subject lined "Does this work?": Chris F. Holm, Jay Stringer, Chad Rohrbacher, Lein Shory.

Thanks to the constant and overwhelming support of the reading and writing community: Benjamin Whitmer, Sean Chercover, John Hornor Jacobs, Hilary Davidson, Brad Parks, Joelle Charbonneau, Owen Laukkanen, Julie Summerell, Keith Rawson, Elizabeth White, Thomas Pluck, Frank Bill, Dan O'Shea, Evil Ray, Art Taylor, Jedidiah Ayres, Cam Ashley, Neil Smith, John McFetridge, Kieran Shea, Brian Lindenmuth, Victor Gischler, Tricia Matthew, Rob Hart, Holly West, Lauren O'Brien, Stephen Blackmoore, Brian Arundel, Matt Funk, Naomi Johnson, Luca Veste, Gerald So, Alison Dasho, Eric Beetner, Nigel Bird, David Cranmer, Dennis Tafoya, Eric Nusbaum, Ray Banks, Jon Jordan, Malachi Stone, Sabrina Ogden, Kent Gowran, Lynn Kostoff, Kat Holm, Drew Smith, Dave White, Scott Phillips, Barna Donovan, Adam Christopher, Jen Forbus, Matthew McBride, Frank Wheeler, Jr., and the 736 more I don't have room to name.

Thanks to my children, Emily and Jack, for many, many reasons.

And thanks to my lovely bride, Helen, for so many more. We did it, babe.

CONTENTS

CHAMPION

"What happened to your face?" Champion Tatum asked his only son.

The boy had been standing in the back doorway, waiting for his father to look up from splitting wood. Champion set the axe down on its head, left the piece of jagged oak where it lay, and crossed the path of hardpacked mud to the back steps.

At ten years old, the boy could have stood on the bottom step and been even with his father, a man who had been beaten enough for the past fifty years. Instead, the boy stayed on the top step, making his father stare up at him, at the scraped chin, little pieces of gravel wedged like flecks of house paint into the skin.

They went inside the house, five rooms that hadn't been cleaned since Eleanor Tatum had come home from the mill late that Saturday night last June, skipped church the next morning, and walked into the front yard to put a bullet through her temple.

"Never seen a woman do that," Champion had overheard one of the deputies saying.

"Must have been pretty messed up, do something like that," a tall man Champion hadn't seen before said. "Women usually take pills. You know, when they cash in."

"Damned shame," another deputy said, shaking his head, scratching into his notepad.

They all shook their heads and agreed it was a damned shame.

Champion looked in the medicine cabinet for a can of antibiotic spray while the boy rinsed the cut out in the sink, washing watery blood and bits of earth down the rust-tinged drain. Champion moved the toothpaste, the cough syrup, the Q-Tips from shelf to shelf. He shut the mirrored door, easing it softly into a metallic click. He reached down below the faucet, held his palm up to catch the water, and splashed it around the basin until it was mostly white again. He wet a washcloth, pulled free some of the loose threads, wadded it into a ball at one end, and dabbed the boy's chin. He set the cloth on the counter, reached under the boy's arms to lift him onto the edge by the sink. Felt the warm strain in his lower back, took a step away from the boy. Told him to hop up on the counter, which the boy did with ease.

"What happened to your face?" Champion asked again, drying the boy's chin with a towel he'd found on the floor.

"I fell."

He nodded. "Looks like it hurt." He put his palms on the boy's ears, tilted the boy's head back to look at the drying blood under the chin.

"'s fine," the boy said. "Just fell is all."

"Reckon the other boy's worse?" he asked, hoping his son had toughened up the last year. Hoping he was back to normal, back to being a boy. Fistfights and forts. Skinning squirrels. Running trot lines. Champion had taken to having an extra few drinks on nights the boy wouldn't stop crying.

The first few days after Eleanor Tatum had killed herself, Champion was the grieving widower, with Tatums from his side, Pennicks from hers, filling up the house. Neighbors came by with food and advice. A day at a time. Be strong for the boy. Call if you need anything. Then a week. A month. Then everyone moved on to the next death in Columbia County. The defensive end at the high school. Too young. A damned shame, they said, then celebrated the boy's life with one Friday night in July at the Legion Hall while Champion and his son sat alone in the darkness. Everyone else had moved on, collecting tragedies like folk tales. Champion woke up each morning, hoping his son was all cried out.

The boy shook his head. The other boy wasn't worse off. No one was worse off. "I had this stick," the boy said. "The walking stick Momma brought back from when she went up to Hot Springs that time."

Champion remembered the time. The curled-up corners of her smile when she'd won employee of the year and they'd sent her up, an all-expense paid vacation for two, to a hotel for the weekend and she and Imogene McAllister had come back with gifts for their families and months' worth of stories to tell. Eleanor had never been as happy as that weekend she was able to "get away," as she'd called it. She'd brought back that walking stick and a marionette for the boy, a pair of boots for her husband. Champion thought about the gifts, but couldn't remember whether she'd brought back anything for herself.

Another boy, Kenny Jenkins's son, had taken the stick away from the boy on the cut-through behind the fishing pond. "He said he'd give it back if I kissed the ground in front of his feet. And I didn't want to start nothing. And there were like four or five boys standing with him and they were all looking at me waiting for me to do something." And this. And that. And. And. And the boy was all alone.

"So I just figured I'd like bend down and . . . " He stopped. Wiped his nose as the tears came, as the cut in his chin reopened.

Champion wet the rag, put it in the boy's hand, pressed the boy's hands to the wound until the boy winced. "Just hold this here. Not too tight," he said. "So you bent down?"

"Yeah, but I wasn't going to kiss the ground," the boy said. "Not for Toby Jenkins or nobody. I just leaned down like I was going to, then I was going to get back up like I'd done it and get my stick back and come home."

"But it didn't work that way, did it?"

"I put my head down and Toby shoved my face into the ground and then everyone goes off laughing."

"It's all right. You're home now."

"I gotta get that stick back, Dad. He took it from me. I gotta get it back." The boy slid down from the counter.

Champion took a roll of toilet paper from the top of the tank, unrolled a couple feet, gave it to the boy to dry his face, blow his nose. Then Champion took the cloth, pressed it to the boy's chin to try to keep the wound closed.

"We'll go in the morning."

"We gotta go now."

"In the morning, son. It's getting late. In the morning."

"You promise?"

Champion was up late watching the Astros give up a three-run lead to the Padres when he heard the boy wake up crying. Give it a minute, Champion told himself. Like he always did. A few minutes later, he told himself to give it a few more minutes. The Astros were up in the ninth with a man on third and one out. Champion heard a storm of noise from the other side of the wall. The boy kicked and cried, trying to exhaust himself to sleep, Champion hoped, but he knew better. He knew the boy was kicking, was swinging in the air. Fighting the emptiness around him.

Champion Tatum stood up, walked into the kitchen, and pulled down what was left of the whiskey. He twisted off the top, downed a couple fingers' worth, then put the top back on and placed the bottle back into the cabinet. Then he stepped out of his boots, turned off the television, and walked into the boy's room. He took a deep breath, closed the door behind him, and climbed into bed with his son, putting the boy's head on his shoulder until the boy fell asleep.

When morning came through the sheets Champion had hung for curtains, he rolled himself off the mattress to the floor. Got to his elbows and knees and worked himself to standing. Next check the government sends, he thought, I'm getting the boy a real bed.

Champion had finished his second cup of coffee when the boy came out of the bathroom, ready to go down the road to the Jenkins house.

They got into the pickup and drove the half mile to see Kenny Jenkins. Champion looked at the distance in silence. Ten years ago I could have walked this no problem, he thought. Maybe twenty.

They pulled into the driveway two minutes later, saw Kenny playing football with his sons, Toby and Wyatt. Kenny tossed the ball back onto the porch as a half-dozen dogs came chasing nothing around the corner of the house. The dogs stopped between the Jenkins boys and the pickup, barking until Kenny threw a stick at them, yelling at the goddamned dogs to shut the hell up.

Champion and the boy got out of the truck and walked across the clumps of weeds and mud. Kenny pulled off his baseball cap, wiped his forehead with the bend of his elbow, put the cap back on.

"Mr. Tatum," he said, "what can I do for you?" He squinted an eye, tilted his head, smiled. Neighborly.

"Seems to have been a problem with the boys yesterday," Champion said, which made Kenny turn to face Wyatt and Toby at his side. "What did you boys do?"

"I didn't do nothing," Toby said.

"I didn't do nothing neither," Wyatt said as they both took a step to the house.

"Probably nothing," Champion said. "One of the boys ended up with my son's walking stick. We just thought we'd save you some trouble and swing by and pick it back up."

Sounded fair, Champion thought. He looked at the man in front of him, half his age and twice his size. A little problem they had, a problem he was helping solve. Probably nothing.

"Hang on a second, Champ," Kenny Jenkins said, taking a step forward. "I know you ain't accusing my boys of stealing." The way he said "Champ," more like a joke than a nickname. Like the way you'd call a puppy "Champ" when he came out of a fight with his ear dangling. Like the way you'd call an old mare "Champ" before you had to put her down.

Champion looked over at his son, who was looking up at him. The boy looked across at the Jenkins boys, then to Mr. Jenkins. "It's okay," the boy whispered to his father. "It's okay."

Champion Tatum took a step toward Kenny Jenkins. "We don't want any trouble," he said. "We just came for the walking stick."

"What if my boys say they don't have your walking stick?" Kenny Jenkins asked, turning his head and spitting across the distance to the side of Champion's shoe. "You gonna apologize for accusing them?"

No one said anything.

Then Champion took a final step to Kenny Jenkins. "Nobody needs any more trouble."

Kenny looked at Champion's eyes. Champion held the stare, searching for his own reflection.

Kenny turned to his sons. "Go get the stick, son," he said to Toby.

"But Dad. I didn't—"

"Get the stick."

+ + +

When they got back to the house, the boy stayed outside with the walking stick, running around the yard, pointing the end of the stick at nothingness, blasting spells into the air.

Champion opened the window in the kitchen, sat down at the table, and listened to his son make explosion sounds as he jumped from stumps along the woods. He thought about what the boy had said on the way back. "You did it. That was great. Did you see his face? That was awesome." And on and on.

In the yard the boy swung the stick around, commanding all his followers to attack the castle.

Inside the empty house, Champion Tatum poured himself the last of the whiskey, thought about the pity he'd seen in Kenny's eyes, and cried for the first time in years.

THE RAVINE

When I came around the corner into his back yard, he had his glasses in his hands, rubbing the lenses with a blue bandana.

I cleared my throat, and he looked up. We were about twenty feet apart.

"The fuck you want, boy?" he said, standing up and grabbing his shotgun from the table. He was more than twice my age, in his mid-60s I'd guess. Thin, rough at the edges. And there were plenty of edges to the guy. Old snakeskin boots. Jeans. Brown flannel shirt hanging out of his pants.

The sun was coming up over the tree line, past the acre-long field behind his house. Midmorning. About this time of year.

"Mr. Greer, my name's Roy Alison." I pulled some papers out of my back pocket.

"I know who you are, shitface." He raised the barrels of the shotgun to my face. "Everybody knows who you are. You're the piece of shit who killed his parents."

That stopped me. I guess I'll never get used to that. Never get away from it. Which is fine. I did kill my parents.

I was sixteen. Sitting in my room. Not bothering anyone. Put on some Blue Oyster Cult. Dropped a couple tabs of pumpkin-head. An hour later my mom busted into my room. My dad had been having kidney trouble a while and had passed out. She didn't want to wait for an ambulance because we were out in the country. And she hated ambulances. Said they were a rip-off. So she loaded my dad into the back seat of the Impala and I was supposed to drive them to the ER. Yeah. Funny story. I thought the oncoming headlights were calling to me. Calling me home. So we all made it to the ER in ambulances. Of course, my mom and dad didn't need ambulances by the time they got there.

I was locked up for a while. Full of the empty darkness, if that makes sense to you. The sort of nothing that fills up everything. Spent the whole time running down the "what if" crap to fill up my soul. What if I hadn't dropped then? What if they'd buckled up? What if this and that? You can go crazy with that. And maybe I did. And maybe when I got out and was all of a sudden an adult and alone, yeah, maybe I did some things I shouldn't have. And maybe those were my fault. But that's the old me. That's not who I am now.

Yeah, I'd had problems. But that was then. All I wanted in my new life was no trouble.

Now I'm working for the county, driving around handing out paperwork, trying to live whatever a normal life is when you're someone with my record, my past. As if anyone is normal.

"I'm here for the county, Mr. Greer." I held the paperwork out for him. "I need to talk to you about your outbuildings. They're not up to code."

He set the gun down on the table and sat back down in his chair, pulled a buck knife from his shirt pocket, and started cutting chunks out of an apple.

He had the same kind of metal lawn chairs we'd had at our house. Light green. Kind of a clamshell. Iron bars folded underneath so you could rock back and forth, humming a little tune to make you think of something else.

"How long you been working for the government?" he asked me.

"Started at the building office last week," I said, still a little nervous looking at the gun, the violence within reach. I had three more visits to make before lunch, so I couldn't waste the whole day here. And I had to get back for a birthday party at the office. I hadn't been a free man for long and this job was the biggest piece of normal I had. My big hope for getting back on track, for keeping the darkness away. "I just need to give you a copy of this report and schedule a time for you to come by the office, Mr. Greer."

"Sit down, son."

"Thank you for the invite, sir, but I need to get moving."

He reached for the gun, then turned it on me, again. "Maybe my polite tone confused you, asshole. Sit the fuck down. I wasn't asking."

I sat down.

Mr. Greer set the shotgun in his lap. Then he ate an apple piece from his blade.

"Wanna tell me how you ended up here?" he asked.

I looked down at the paper, like I was reading something. "We got a call. Tip. Said you were breaking the zoning ordinance."

He shook his head, spit out part of the apple. "Not that, you dipshit. I know that. I made the call. I mean how you got here." He emphasized the last word, looked around the property.

He made the call? Why would he make the call? "I'm sorry, Mr. Greer. I don't understand."

"Here. How did you end up here? Where you are now?"

Ten seconds or so went by. Felt like longer. I wasn't sure what he was talking about, but I figured I had to say something. "Google Maps. Took 79 through Emerson. Turned a couple miles out, down that a ways until I hit what I guess was a logging road. You're all alone back here."

"Yeah. I'm all alone." He folded his knife back into his shirt pocket and stood. He looked up to his outbuildings at the back of his property. "'We live as we dream—alone.' That's from a book, son." He grabbed the shotgun and walked over to me. When I started to stand he put the barrels of the gun against my chest. "I was asking how you got here. Walking around like a free man. After you killed your parents that night. After you killed my daughter."

My arms were at my sides and I wasn't even close to ready when the butt of the gun hit my jaw and knocked me cold.

I'd given up drinking a few years ago. Drugs a year before that when I was back behind bars. And I tried not to cuss. Tried not to speed. Tried to live a good life now. Make up for what I'd done.

"No reason you should know me," Mr. Greer was saying. Mid-conversation. Like he'd been talking for a while. But I was just coming back around. I rubbed my jaw where he'd hit me. Scratched through my beard. Something was flaking there. Blood. Dirt. I blinked. Rubbed my eyes with my hands, which were tied together. "She kept saying how it was so sad, such darkness." He was running a sharpening wheel, sparks flying off the knife blade. I looked out through the windows but only saw sky. I was pretty sure we were in one of the outbuildings I'd come to complain about. Yeah. Another funny story. "You know anything about darkness, shithead?"

Yeah. I had some ideas. Some ideas I tried to stay away from. "I didn't kill your daughter."

"The hell you didn't," he said. "You kill everything, don't you? People like you? You're a curse. A blight. A bringer of darkness."

For what must have been the twentieth time in the past however long I'd been at his place, I had no idea what he was talking about. "I didn't kill your daughter."

Looking through the windows, I could see the sun at the top of the sky. Guess I'd been out a little while, but not too long.

He stopped sharpening the knife and turned around to face me. "Maybe you should stop talking about my daughter right about now."

I'd wanted this job. I'd wanted to work outside. Drive around, listening to Drive-By Truckers, Stevie Ray Vaughan, Little Feat, all windows-down and fields full of sunshine. Sounds like a great day, back roads through Columbia County, grabbing a sandwich at the gas station, being your own boss in a sense. Staying away from trouble. Living a normal life.

Yeah, I'd done things I wasn't proud of. The accident with my parents. A few other things that ended up with people dying. Put a man down in self-defense. Finished a fight I hadn't started. The neck is a fragile twig. But I'd served my time for some of that and that was behind me. Someone else's life. Not who I'd wanted to be, who I'd become. I knew that if I lived clean from here on out, woke up every morning in the light, things would be fine. I was starting from scratch. Only this point on counts. A good job. Coworkers. Friends. The sunlight. The glare from the road. The summer brightness of things not yet destroyed.

He had me up, blade at the back of my neck, pushing me out the door to the edge of a ravine behind his field. He hit me in the shoulder with the hilt of the knife, and I dropped to my knees.

"My girl was impressionable," he said. "Young. Innocent." He sounded like he was going to cry, sniffling a little. But he didn't. Just stood there looking out at the ravine. "What you did to your parents sent her over the edge. She was young. Troubled. Artistic. Like her mother." He pointed the knife at one of the other sheds. Another cinderblock box that brought me out here in the first place. I was sluggish from the head shots, but I focused where he pointed.

"That one there," he said. "With the lock on the door. Full of her paintings." I wasn't talking, so he kept on. "She did thirty-seven paintings of you and your mommy and daddy. The car crash. Locked herself in her room and painted. And screamed and cried. And painted. All 'cause of you and your goddamned fool life. Broke her soul."

"I didn't kill your daughter."

"Damn sure did." He walked to the edge of the ravine and looked down. "She couldn't take it. The emptiness. The darkness. Whatever it is these kids feel. I just tried to get her through it after her mother died. Just hoping she'd be okay. Hope." He spit. "Damn hope."

"I'm sorry about your daughter, but I didn't kill her. I've done a lot of bad things, but I didn't kill her." Back here was dark, muddy, seeping through the knees of my pants.

"I been watching you. Waiting for you. Thought I was gonna have to come after you. Then I hear you're working for the county now that you're a free man. Made a call. And here you are. Come to deliver paperwork. Just like the social services people when they took Lily away. They take your daughter and give you forms. Then they come back and tell you she ate a bottle of pills. And then there's all that other paperwork to bury her." He walked up to me, put the point of the knife to my neck. "You killed her. Sent her over the edge."

I tried to hold my head still as I talked. "Not my fault."

I could carry the blame for a lot of stuff. But not this. All I wanted was a new start. Fresh on the job. A blank slate.

He put the heel of his boot into my chest, my breath falling in sputters on the ground. "You took my daughter from me, you piece of shit. After all those years. The past is the past. But you never get out of it. You can let it go all you want, boy, but it ain't up to you. It don't let go of you."

I thought he was talking about me. What I'd done. My parents. The time I'd spent in juvie. The week I was free before I'd been pushed around enough and went out looking for a fight and found it. The year and a half I went inside for the stabbing. Trouble inside. More trouble outside. Six months at Haven House, then on my own.

I was facedown on the ground, trying to push myself up. "Trouble's a dog, son. A goddamned fucking dog. It gets your scent and hunts you down." I thought he was talking about me.

He wasn't.

"Yeah, I did some shit I ain't proud of. Some 'fucked-up, repugnant shit.' That's from a movie, son." I was still struggling to get up, and he kicked my arms out from under me. I fell back into the dirt, hit the side of my head on a rock, something hidden just below the dark ground. "I thought I was clear. That I'd left it behind. Then Claudia, that's my wife, she gets sick and leaves. Then Lily gets depressed because of your stupid shit. Says there ain't no point anymore." He looked at the buildings that held her paintings. "She got artistic. Woman at her school said that was good. An outlet." He spit. "Outlet, my ass."

He walked over to me. He was close enough that I could snap his neck, but I was past that. I was good now. I could get through this without violence. Let him talk. Let him free himself. Let him come through the pain, the broken glass in the belly like I had. Just let him talk.

"You understand what I'm saying to you?" He leaned into my ear. "Can you hear me?"

He turned his back on me, but I didn't have the strength to get up. My eye was covered in dirt and blood. My head was liquid, moving around, looking for balance.

Five years ago I could have taken out his knee in a couple of seconds, sent an elbow into his Adam's apple. Five years ago that is what I did. What sent me back inside. I didn't want to go back inside. And I didn't want that, that darkness he was talking about, back inside of me. If you've never felt it, then you don't know what I'm talking about. The darkness that fills in from the edges. You think you can hold it back, but it seeps through like mud through door cracks.

He turned around to look at me. Take the knife, then I could settle him down. Talk to him. I didn't want to have to break him. I didn't want that life back.

"Claudia gone. Lily gone. All payback, son. For the shit I'd done when I was a young man." He shook his head. "It comes after you. Takes a while, but it finds you." He kneeled down near my face. "Like I found you. And that's what I'm gonna do. You see, some people get bit by a dog and they get scared of dogs. They run and hide. Wet their pants when a dog barks." He spit. "And some people, well, son, some people get mad at the fucking dog. Some people get real fuckin' pissed at the dog. And some people find that dog and carve a fuckin' hole in that piece of shit's head to clean out the darkness."

He aimed the knife at me, reached back into his belt for a pistol in the other hand. "You're not the first piece of shit I've had to settle a score with." He looked at me, then down to the bottom of the ravine. "You know how many bodies they've found down there?"

I didn't say anything, kept my eyes on his. Tried to fight the desire to send my head into his jaw.

He said it again. "You know how many bodies they've found down there?" He leaned down into my face. "Not a goddamned one."

I stood up, heart beating, filling my ears with thumps and blood. I was good now. The pressure coming back, again. I'd given up drugs. Pressing against the inside of my skull. I didn't even cuss anymore. Pushing and pulling. Filling me. I could feel the blood moving out from my chest into my arms, my thighs. "I didn't kill your daughter."

My hands were still tied, which was fine. I didn't need much freedom anymore.

+ + +

I got back to the office in time for lunch. A birthday cake was there for Shirley. Her fortieth, so it was all black with balloons here and there in the office.

When I walked in through the side door, everyone stopped and looked up at me. The mud on my pants, dark stains on my arms. The painting I was holding. A ravine filled with darkness.

My boss, Jerry, stood up, walked toward me, and asked me if I'd had any problems that morning.

"Problems?" I asked. I shook my head, wiped my palms on my shirt. "Not a goddamned one."

PURPLE HULLS

"What are you making?" I asked my grandmother that afternoon. The heat outside was like a layer of the sun pressing down on us, and we'd picked purple hull peas until we'd filled all the baskets we had.

We'd walked across the fields back to her house, climbed up the cement steps, and used our elbows and chins to open the thin-metal screen door. A sprig from a dying nandina bush had gotten caught in the door. I'd reached back, snapped the branch like a finger, then closed the door behind me.

My grandmother had gotten old, bleach-stained sheets from the back room, the one my mother grew up in, the room she kept sealed like a tomb now, and spread the sheets on the floor. She'd picked up some cross-stitch from the seat as she sat down into her chair. "A little Christmas sampler for Ettie May," she said. Then she pressed a button and the chair lowered her to a sitting position. She closed her eyes, took a deep breath. Maybe said a little prayer.

We shelled purple hull peas for an hour, popping the peas out of their shells, staining my fingers purple. She didn't talk about the car crash that had killed my parents so many years ago. How it had been my fault. How she missed them every day. She didn't talk about how we'd gone fifteen years after the funeral without seeing each other. How this was the fifth weekend in a row we'd been together, making up for lost time since I was trying to put things right, trying to fix what that one night had sent to pieces.

"So you still working for the county? Government work? Nice office job?"

I said I wasn't. "Kinda went downhill quick," I said. She nodded like she knew. Like she was fine with whatever happened. I said I was planning to look for something down in Springhill, up in Magnolia.

She didn't talk about the letters on her kitchen table behind me. The ones that said she was in default. Past due. She didn't talk about the reverse mortgage, the bad investments. The man at the bank.

She tossed some purple shells my way. "You got to get to them before they go full purple or they're too tough," she said. "Don't let them dry up on the vine. Snap 'em right off."

I said okay.

"There's a sweet spot," she said. "Couple days when they're just right. Keep at it. You'll learn."

But I wouldn't. That's not the way things work out.

She turned on the radio, and we listened to a replay of a show at the Louisiana Hayride. They were talking about a guitar player. A retrospective. Local boy made good. James Burton. I didn't recognize the name.

"That Burton boy," my grandmother said. "Had a talent. Played with Elvis Presley. That Ricky Nelson, too."

I was running out of peas, so I pulled some from her basket.

"Made music with his hands," she said. "Work with your hands, Roy. Best thing for a young man like you. Make something. Make something of yourself."

She wasn't talking to me anymore. She was just talking.

I stood up and got us some sweet tea from a heavy pitcher. Boiled the water until it had soaked up all the sugar, all the sweetness it could handle. The hotter it gets, the more sweet it holds. Up to a point. Then it all falls apart.

I looked at a framed picture she'd nailed to the wall. A faded, square Kodak photograph from the early '70s. Me and my mom and dad, all covered in sweat and pasted with dirt from cleaning up the storage barn in the back. I was five or six in the picture and I remembered the pants, how they didn't come down far enough. They had a patch on the knee, a yellow piece of cloth my mom had used to cover the hole I'd made flipping a bicycle down a flight of sidewalk steps in Magnolia. Little pieces of thread holding it all together, so many years ago.

I pulled back the curtains and watched an oil truck drive toward someone else's property.

In back of the house were things that were boxed up after my parents died. I looked up through the door. Someday I'd have to sort through everything.

The show ended, and the news people talked before they changed to jazz. My grandmother talked about the news. A smash and grab. Breaking and entering. House fire in Minden. "Why don't they ever tell you about the good news? Always negative. What is this place coming to?"

I said I didn't know. She hummed along to some big band tune and leaned her head back.

I pulled the sheet outside and cleaned up the hulls, put the peas away for her while she fell asleep in the chair. I sorted her mail, shut the window to keep her safe. I put one of the bank letters in my pocket.

I made a little noise moving a chair to wake her up, then walked across the room to kiss her goodbye. She pressed a button and the chair my cousins paid for lifted her a little so that I caught her on the eyeball instead of the forehead. I told her I'd see her next weekend and left.

✦ ✦ ✦

That Wednesday I met Cleovis in the old Magic Mart parking lot and got into his truck. I asked if he was still cool with the plan. He said he was.

"But you know this won't fix anything," he said.

"Yeah," I said, looking across the empty lot. "Nothing ever does."

On the way to the man's house, I looked at my face in the side mirror. Like watching someone on a television show you weren't used to.

Cleo turned the radio to a pop country station and smacked his palms on the steering wheel, drumming along.

We got to the man's house and walked around, making sure he was alone. He was wearing sweatpants and a robe when he opened the door.

"Can I help you?" he asked, looking at Cleo, then at me.

I told him who we were looking for, and he asked again whether he could help us. So I showed him the letter from the bank.

"Look," he said, "I don't know what this is about, but I am no longer affiliated with that establishment, so if you have business to conduct, please contact my replacement."

He talked to us like he was writing us another letter.

When he tried to close the door, I stepped into his house and broke his nose with the heel of my hand. He reached up to cover his face and I put the toe of my work boot into his balls.

Cleo closed the door behind us as the man hit the floor and tried crawling backward. He wasn't fast enough. Cleo locked the door and turned off the porch light.

I talked to the man for a few minutes about his job, about how it was wrong of him to deal with people the way he was. How people can only take so much until they have to do something.

He said something about the entire industry being in turmoil. Derivatives. Regulations. Cash flow. I thought about what my grandmother had said about James Burton, about making something with your hands.

I put the man's forehead into his granite counter a few times until he almost passed out.

The man sat on his kitchen floor, sniffling blood up his nose, then coughing it out. Then shaking, crying. He asked why we were there. He said his brother was an army captain and would be back soon. He said he had a safe upstairs with money. He said a lot of stuff just trying to hold things together.

I told him how my grandmother worked for years after my grandfather died just to pay for the house. I told him how she knitted caps for every newborn in the hospital. I told him how she jarred pickles each year so that the needy at her church pantry had something besides just canned soups.

Then I thought about what this man had done to my grandmother. About what had happened to my parents. About how that was my fault. About how I think about that every day. About how nothing I will ever do will make it right. How you make one mistake when you're not even thinking and everything falls apart. And nothing can patch that. Nothing can make that right. Nothing ever goes back on the vine.

I looked down at the man, spilling blood and spit onto his kitchen tiles.

Cleo picked him up off the floor. I pulled a chair from the dining room table and helped him tie the man to it.

Then I thought about making things with my hands. The making. The unmaking.

THIS TOO
SHALL PASS

"The stars," she said. "See how close together they are? Almost touching? Look." She took his fingers, pressed them together to hold a star. "You can almost touch one to another. Feel the light, one against the other. The fire."

He said okay. Sure.

She rolled back into the dark field.

"But then you get close," she said, "and it turns out they're millions and millions of miles away. Did you know that?"

He said he didn't.

"The closest star, I mean one to another, the closest one is like a hundred million light years from the next one, like in the whole universe. And the closer you get to a star, like they look close together now, but if you were to fly up there, all that way, the closer you get to the stars, the further away you are from the next one. The further away everything is."

He said he didn't know that, either. He closed his eyes, thought about the tips of her fingers on his, pressing together. The flat of her thumb against the knuckle of his. The tip of her index finger guiding his. He'd seen a movie, maybe a documentary, and a soldier had stepped on a land mine in the desert darkness. Had both his legs blown off. And he woke up, still feeling the legs. Still feeling the weight. It was called a "phantom" something. Feeling it pressed against you. He wondered how long that could last.

He heard something. Something deep. Something throbbing. Then a little light in the distance. Like stars on the ground. Only not stars. Not stars, at all. He looked across to see wavy shadows moving in and out of the light as people were coming toward them, getting bigger the closer they came.

"Staci," one of the guys said. They were all wearing their red football jerseys, jeans, boots. "You all right?"

"Yeah," she said, wiping her mouth with the back of her hand. "I think . . . " She swallowed. "I think those Jello shots put me over the edge. Somebody oughta check those."

Rusty sat watching. No one said anything to him.

One of them reached a hand down for Staci. Then they walked away, toward the house, their football jerseys shining in the moonlight, the stars, the house lights. Everything reflecting off them.

Alone in the field, he watched everything move further away.

Jake found Rusty sitting on the steps to the house, back turned to the party.

"Hey, man, you been out here all this time? Thought you were going to take a piss."

Rusty rocked back and forth a little, legs pulled close. "Tripped over Staci out in the field."

"No kidding? What was she doing out there? Taking a piss, too?"

"Yeah," Rusty said. "I guess she was." He stood up, moved his head from side to side, couldn't get his neck to crack. "You see the stars?"

Jake smushed his lips together, raised an eyebrow. "The stars?" He looked up. "Uh, yeah. Stars."

"I wonder who names them all."

"Hell if I know," Jake said, shaking his head. "Imagine they're all named by now. Hey, remember when Boone Crawford said his daddy went to the moon, came back with a moon rock?"

Rusty laughed. "Oh, yeah. What was that? Second grade?"

"No. I didn't move over until third, so it had to be third or fourth, I guess."

"Man, that was some funny shit. He was so damn proud of that. Remember when he brought it to school?"

"And Robbie and Moe and those guys busted it into tiny pieces and Boone goes crying to Coach Womack?"

Rusty laughed along with Jake, but it all seemed less funny than it had at the time. Rusty hadn't thought about that in years. Now he felt a little guilty for laughing. "Still can't believe about him and his mom."

"Who?"

"Boone."

"Oh," Jake said, stopped laughing. "Yeah. Well his daddy was always a crazy fucker, you know?"

"Yeah."

"I mean, what are you gonna do, right?"

Right, Rusty thought. What are you gonna do?

✦ ✦ ✦

When they got back to the house, Jake said he was going to look for some beer. Rusty said fine.

The house had a screened-in porch. Your basic four-room farmhouse, emptied when the Campbells left a couple of months before. Behind the four rooms, a mud porch and the bathroom, which didn't work. On the door, Rusty had seen before, someone had written "out of order" in marker on the door. Added below, in pen, "so's your momma."

Jake was probably in the mud porch now, where the kegs were. Living room to the right. Dining to the left. Behind those rooms, kitchen and bedroom. Your basic four-room farmhouse. Only the farm gone, fields given over to weeds and hay and scrub pines and, a half mile from the house, near the road, a couple of roadkill deer he'd noticed when he and Jake had driven up an hour before. Then he'd walked around, wondering when they could leave. Then he saw Staci walking out the back door and he waited for some idiot to follow after her.

After a minute, he told himself he was just worried about her. Nothing weird about that. He wanted to make sure she was all right. She was his friend, after all. They'd grown up together. Same school. Same church. They'd talked a thousand times. Maybe they could be more than friends. Not now, of course. But some day. After the awkward stage. He and his mom were watching one of those "Before They Were Stars" shows the other day. He saw how they were when they were his age. He knew. Like his mom said whenever something went wrong, "This too shall pass."

Jake came back with a red plastic cup of foamy beer in each hand. "You just going to stand around here all night?" He handed Rusty a beer, then elbowed him. "We gotta mingle with the chickies."

Rusty was standing in the doorway, watching Staci McMahen look out the window as though she were waiting for something.

"Nice night," he thought about saying.

Then what would she say? "Yes, it is." Then he'd be stuck, again.

What if he just walked up to her and said something real. Something like, "Don't you ever get tired of all this fake stuff?"

And maybe she'd say "What fake stuff?" and he'd be able to tell her. Or maybe he wouldn't.

Or maybe she'd say she was tired of it, too. Of everyone trying to act like everyone else. Copying the pack leader. He'd seen a movie at school about that. Mimicking behavior. And maybe they could talk about that. How wouldn't it be better just to go out, lie down under the stars, and talk about, well, what? What did he have to talk about with her? He couldn't stand the music she listened to, but maybe she couldn't, either. Maybe if she would just walk out to the field with him again, he could tell her about the songs he liked. About the words. About how real they were. About how real everything could be if they could just have that moment back, let it carry on, staring at the stars until they blurred across the darkness, edging into each other.

He took a deep breath, then a step forward. Then he moved back to the doorway. He took another breath and was waiting to move when Loriella walked across the room, grabbed Staci by the arm, and pulled. "C'mon, we're heading out to the spooklight."

The story had been there before any of them. Long ago, on a night just like this one, the Georgia Southern bound for Texarkana had stopped near the Walkerville Cemetery to let another train pass. The young brakeman, about to be married, walked around the cars, checking the couplings and reading a letter from his sweetheart. The wind kicked up a little, just the thought of a breeze, and blew one of the sheets under the back car. He looked under, but couldn't find it. The day was getting dark quickly, much like today, and he lit a lantern, then looked back under the car for the letter. He found it between the tracks, wedged under part of a tie. He reached across and the car rolled back, slicing through his neck, sending his body down the hill, the letter into the wind. When the night comes up quickly, like tonight, you can see the brakeman, lighting his lantern and walking along the train line down near Walkerville, looking for the lost page of the letter.

When Rusty finished telling the story, Jake cocked an eyebrow. "Shouldn't he be looking for his head? Shit, how's he looking for anything?"

"I think maybe he got his head back," Rusty said.

"You mean like he found it under the train? Or like when he died and shit, like it magically reappeared like in spirit form?"

"Yeah, I guess. Something like that." Rusty looked down the road to where all the taillights had gone as he and Jake and a handful of others stayed at the house.

"It's just a light, then. Just floating out in the darkness?"

"Yeah."

"And what? People get all scared of it? Like a ghost?"

"Yeah. Like it's just sitting there, then it's moving. And you're just watching the light there at the other end of the tracks."

"I bet it scares the shit outta the chicks, right?"

"I guess," Rusty said. "I don't know."

"So, you want to go or what? We can follow them or whatever."

Rusty walked to the side of the house as Jake followed him. He looked at the darkness where he and Staci McMahen had been. He looked up at the sky, for the stars covered now by cloud film.

He looked back down the dirt road, where it cut through other people's woods. He walked toward the road, toward the tree line, saw the orange-pink moon rising into a hazy darkness and closed his eyes.

GOOD TIMES GONE

Clint Womack sat on an upturned milk crate, back against the open door, looking out across the creek that ran through town, from the bayou out east, through ravine and under bridges, until it drained away, forgotten in someone else's fields.

He folded the letter from the court clerk into his shirt pocket. He'd gone through three cigarettes already and was about to start the fourth when Bethann Roberson cleared her throat and stepped outside.

He'd been avoiding talking to her all morning, ever since the store manager had told him to fire "one of the new ones." Bethann, he'd meant. Or Tyler Crawford. They'd both started on the same day in March. "Last in, first out" was as good a policy as any he'd figured when he'd gotten the news of the cutbacks. Then he got to thinking about how they did the opposite with the milk. With the cheese. With pretty much everything else in the store. The more recent to come in gets put to the back, so the customer would always pull out the oldest first. The July 19 milk was in front, six cartons ahead of the July 24 milk. All the way through the store, he thought, except for the people.

Truth be told, he'd nearly fired Bethann that morning. They'd already let go Jimmy from meats, as well as a few cashiers, on

36

Monday. They all had family insurance, so getting them off the books was a significant savings, his boss, Ron, had said, adding how that didn't play into the decision, you understand. Clint said that he did.

"You got a minute?" Bethann asked. "I got something to ask you."

Clint said "Yeah," knowing that nothing good ever follows that. What people mean is that they have something important to ask you and want you to pay attention. Something important to them, is what they mean. And they want you to set the beer down, turn the game off, and pay attention to them. To their needs. Because you don't have any needs.

Bethann started to say something, then drew her breath back in. "Well, me and Tyler and Rhonda were back here yesterday and we were talking about the mound back there." Bethann pointed to a hill behind the store, near where the bowling alley used to be. "It true what they say about Dumbo Mountain?"

"What do they say?"

"They buried an elephant there?"

Clint broke the filter off another cigarette, put the flush end in his mouth, spun the wheel of his lighter until it caught. "Yeah. We sure as hell did." He flicked the filter along the outside wall.

"You did?"

"Yeah," Clint said. "We all did. Huge damn thing. Hardly see it now. Shit, that was a long time ago." He pulled the cigarette out, lifted the bottom of his apron, and wiped the sweat from under his chin.

"So what? He just dropped dead? In the circus?"

"Something like that."

"Wow. No shit," she said. "I thought they were just making it up, you know."

Clint nodded, leaned his head back onto the door. Looked up at the "Not An Exit" sign bent crooked above his head. "Weighed two tons. Had to dig a hole fifteen, twenty feet deep."

"Damn. So what happened? Somebody feed him from the discount meat bin?"

Clint grinned, leaned forward on the milk crate. "He was putting up the tent. Or she. Whatever. The trainer was riding her, pulling up this big metal pole for the middle of the tent. The pole hits a wire and zap, fried elephant. Then the elephant falls over, crushes the guy riding her. Dead trainer. Think it fried some other guy, too."

"Holy crap. When was this?"

"In the '80s, I guess. '84. '85."

"Before my time. We didn't move to Springhill 'til I was ten. Around '98? '99."

"Yeah, it was definitely mid-'80s. Late teens for me." Young and summer careless, riding up and down Main just like the kids still did. From a parking lot at one end of town to a parking lot at the other. Grab an Icee, "enhance" with cheap vodka, drive around until it's time to fight or screw. He closed his eyes, leaned back again. "Took us all day to bury her. They had to get a big wrecker, pull the elephant off the trainer." He tightened his neck, shuddered. "Damn mess."

"Yeah, I imagine. Not like a mountain or nothing anymore. But it is weird."

"Was about ten feet tall, I guess, once we did it. Had to put all this lime on there too, cover the elephant. Health department said it would help eat away at the thing."

Clint thought about telling her how after that day, he'd climb to the top of the hill while everyone else was in front of the buildings, driving around the parking lots. How he'd sit there and watch cars go up and down the roads, seeing people jump from one truck to the other, stand in the truck beds wailing down Main Street while someone played a tape of AC/DC or Van Halen. How once he'd been waiting under the awning of the Dairy Freeze after Georgie Porterfield kicked him out so Georgie could hook up with Jolene Campbell. Remembering how when she'd come over to Georgie's car, Clint had thought she was coming to talk to him. How she opened the door on his side and how Georgie had said just wait there, that he and Jolene would be back. And how they'd driven out to the Little League field, then cruised back by twenty minutes later, honking and flashing their lights. And how he'd had to get a ride home from Mrs. Dalton, who was on her way back from working at the mill.

Now Georgie was dead. Car wreck. And Jolene was married now. And so was Clint, at least until the final paperwork was done. Then he'd be single, again. And then what? Join a reading club? Online dating? Damn, how much would all that cost?

"So what happened? They do the circus without the elephant?"

"What?" Clint blinked his way back. "Yeah. Didn't want to disappoint the kids. They couldn't get the tent up, so we just had it outside. Seems like not many people showed up for it, though."

For the past week, Clint had been trying to count the number of single women he knew. He hadn't been to church in more than a year, but he'd have to start back there. He tried to remember when the singles' Bible study was at Macedonia. Maybe it was Thursdays, after choir practice. Maybe there was someone he could ask. Maybe he could look at schedules online at the library, visit a couple churches each week.

"I wanted to ask you something else," Bethann said.

Or maybe the answer was here. Maybe someone he worked with. Bethann. Or Monica in the front office. They didn't get rid of Monica, did they? Maybe after he fired Bethann or Tyler, he'd see about talking to Monica.

"Ron said I should talk to you since you're the department manager. It's just that, I mean, I know there've been a bunch of changes and I was just hoping that, well, I mean, I was just wondering if maybe Tyler and I could keep working on the same shift like we've been doing?"

"Same shift? With Tyler?" Clint picked up his cigarette from the ground.

"Right. I mean, we've sorta started to go out and all. I guess everybody knows by now. But it's like, if he's working early and I'm working late and all, then, I mean, we just want to be able to see each other, you know, like socially." She took a breath and waited. She'd practiced the speech, probably in the bathroom mirror in the stock room.

One of them had to go. Clint didn't make that part of the decision. The only choice he had was which one it would be. "Shouldn't you be going back on shift?"

"Oh," she said. "I thought I'd go back in when you finished your break."

"This is my lunch."

"Oh, sorry about that. Yeah. Okay."

When she turned to go, Clint told her to send Tyler back to see him.

The keys clinked in the bowl by his front door as Clint hit the remote in stride to the refrigerator. He pulled out his last beer, grabbed a couple pieces of cheese, and sat down on his couch to watch whatever was on TV.

He was drifting in and out after another fifteen-hour shift, hearing the infomercial, the second bottle of skin cream at no extra cost, simply for trying. Just pay separate shipping and handling. He was sitting on top of Dumbo Mountain, talking to

Bethann Roberson, who turned into Jolene Campbell, then back. They were pouring tubs of white cream onto the hill to make it go away, to make everything okay. Below them, in the parking lot, someone was putting up a tent. He walked down and saw a revival going on, with people he recognized. He knew he was late for the revival. He should have been there that morning. In the dream, he looked around for help, then realized no one there knew him. A man at the front banged a gavel to call the meeting to order. And banged. And banged.

Clint woke to a voice. A woman's voice. "Hello." Then more knocking.

"Oh, hi, Mrs. Richardson. I was just—" he started saying as he opened the front door.

"Clint, I'm sorry to bother you, but I'm selling tickets for the fundraiser and I was hoping I could count on you and Eileen showing up."

"Sure. I'd invite you in, but it's kind of a mess right now." He looked back and noticed the magazines, blankets, fried chicken boxes spread around.

"Oh, that's not a problem," she said, walking past him.

He closed the door behind her. "Me and Eileen, we aren't together anymore."

"Oh, I'm sorry to hear that. I hope everything is okay?" she said like a question.

"She just . . . " he said, then stopped. "I don't know. We're just not together."

"Well, maybe it's for the best. The Lord works in mysterious ways."

"Yes, ma'am. You were saying something about tickets?"

"Oh, yes." She reached into her purse and pulled out her glasses. "Lose my head if it weren't screwed on. Let's see. The tickets. For the fundraiser. How many should I put you down for?"

"What fundraiser?"

"For the McMahen girl. Walt and Flo's daughter. You know, the one what went missing."

"Fundraiser?"

"The concert. The Dorcheat Dirt Band? It's been on the radio. To raise money for the reward."

"To find the girl?"

"Yes, to find the girl." June Richardson sighed, put her glasses back in her purse, saw the bottle of beer on the coffee table, and shook her head. "Should I come back by when you're sober?"

"I'm fine, Mrs. Richardson. It's just been a long day."

"Well it's been a long day for Staci McMahen's family, too. A long three days."

"I'm sure it has. I'm sorry."

"I knew that Pribble boy was trouble, all that drug dealing with Clay Sawyer and the lot of them. You know, I told Flo that last year, but I'm not one to say 'I told you so.' Could be the Alison boy, I suppose. His grandma lives up there, you know."

"Pribble?"

"That whole family is bad news. Isn't your sister dating one of them?"

"MeChell? To be honest with you, I don't know. I haven't, I mean . . . "

"You just tell her to watch herself. It's like the Bible says, 'The devil comes like a thief in the night.' We have to do what we can or we'll have another Bobo Shinn and no one wants that."

"Bobo Shinn? That Magnolia woman, got kidnapped back in the '80s?"

"Summer of '78. Never found her. And we'll not have that happen this time. Those poor Shinns. We have to offer a big reward. And investigators. And advertisements on the TV. And that costs money. And that's why we're back to the fundraiser. Now, how many tickets can I put you down for?"

Clint reached into his front pocket, felt the fifty cents he had left over from the Coke machine. Reached onto the coffee table for his wallet and opened it up. "How much are the tickets?"

"They're $20 each or two for $35. Tickets will not be available at the door," she recited, "so you'd best buy now."

Clint looked at the edge of the ATM receipt he'd gotten when he tried to pull $50 out of his account and found out he had all of $38 in the bank. "I'm afraid I don't have any cash on me."

"We'll take a check. Just make it out to the VFW Women's Auxiliary."

Clint bit his lip.

She smiled. "You can just put 'VFW Aux' on it. No one can spell it."

"I'm not sure where my checkbook is."

"Clint Womack, if you're just brushing me off so you can buy your tickets from your sister, you should just tell me now."

"My sister?"

"Billy has the whole insurance office selling for him. He really wants that steak dinner Wiley's offered up for whoever sells the most tickets."

"MeChell. Yeah. That's it. I was supposed to buy them from her. I'm sorry."

June Richardson put the tickets and sales sheet back in her purse. "Well, you could have just told me that. I would have understood."

"I'm sorry. I'm just—"

"Drunk?"

"Tired."

She moved to the door. "By the way, Albert and I were listening to your cousin on the baseball game. That Justin is something special. I bet your whole family is proud of what he's done with his life."

+ + +

"Webster Insurance, where we protect what you love. MeChell speaking."

"Hey, sis."

"Hey, Clint. Long time no hear."

"Yeah, sorry about that."

"You okay?"

"Yeah. Fine."

"Did you need something?"

"No, I just . . . "

"Are you okay? I mean, after, you know."

"Oh, yeah. I'm fine. It's final next week. Got the paperwork from the clerk's office. I'll be single again."

"I'll pass word to lock up the ladies."

He laughed. "Right. Speaking of ladies, is Tammy Sanders still working there?"

"Yes," she said, and Clint could tell she was cupping the phone, talking softly. "It's Tammy Adams now."

"Oh."

"That why you called? Looking for a date?"

"Not really. I don't guess."

"Well?"

"I don't know. I was just talking to a woman about some dirt band fundraiser."

"Sorry, bro. I'm plumb out of tickets. Sold the last pair to Skinny Dennis this morning."

"No, I was just, this woman was saying how the girl went missing."

"Staci McMahen. I know. Isn't it awful? Can you imagine? How terrible is that?"

"Yeah, it's pretty bad, yeah. She said that the girl had been going out with one of the Pribbles."

"Danny? Yeah. I think Marlene mentioned that."

"She said you were going out with one of the Pribbles, too."

"Dwayne."

"I guess." Clint counted off a few seconds of silence. "You still there?"

"I'm here."

"Well?"

"Well, what?"

"Well, I was just wondering if you were still going out with him."

"Who I date is none of your business, little brother."

"I know, I just, you know." He shifted the phone from one ear to the other, then back. "I don't know."

She took a deep breath into the phone. "Dwayne and I are no longer an item, if you must know. Though it isn't any of your business."

"Okay."

"Clint, are you okay? You sound weird."

"Weird?"

"Like lost. Distracted."

"Yeah, I don't know. I'm fine. Just a lot going on."

"You need to talk about it?"

"It's fine. Don't worry about it."

"Clint, if this is about the divorce, I mean, just think about Mom and Dad. How miserable they were and then when they got divorced, how much happier they were."

"They were always happy. Everything was fine."

"No. You don't remember. You were too young. They were miserable."

"No, they weren't."

"Okay."

"They were happy. They were always happy. Everything was fine."

"Okay. Okay. I can come over at lunch. Or tonight. We can have dinner. It's girls' night out, but I can—"

"It's cool. I have to work late anyway."

"I can treat. It's no trouble."

"Hey, Clint. Can I talk to you for a second?"

Clint finished tying his apron, picked up the price gun, and walked toward Ron's office. "Sure, boss. What you need?"

"Just need to have a quick chat," Ron said, moving behind the folding card table he used for a desk. "Close the door behind you."

Clint sat down, rubbed a $1.49 pink sticker onto the inside of his index finger. "What you need?"

"Clint, as you know, we've been making some changes around here."

Clint nodded.

"This is a tough economy. Consumer confidence, right? The big chains. The competition. All the regulations. Things like that, you know?"

Clint nodded. Looked up at the wall behind Ron at the wood-mounted photographs of the Little League teams the grocery store had sponsored through the years, the faces he couldn't quite make out.

"So, as you know, we've been making some changes around here," Ron said. "And we've had to make some difficult choices here. Not choices, really. I mean, if we had a choice, maybe. But we don't have a choice. We have to do what we have to do. Nobody is happy about any of this. Is this making any sense?"

"Are you trying to fire me, Ron?"

Ron laughed. "No, no. It's just that, we're rolling out some furloughs. Time off. You can think of it as a vacation. An extra three weeks in the next six months."

"Extra vacation?"

"Well, not vacation per se. It's three weeks of furlough. Unpaid leave. We all have to take it. Even I have to take it."

"Even you, huh?"

"All of us. We're a team. We have to band together. Take one for the team, you know. Knuckle down and fight hard. Things aren't like they were when we were kids. Tough times."

"They used to have carnivals in the parking lot."

"Carnivals? I don't understand."

"Circus, I guess. Right here. In the front parking lot. Back in the '70s and '80s. The Shriners or Jaycees put it on for the kids, give us something to do. Good times back then."

"I think I heard something about that."

"It was before you moved here, I imagine."

"Yes. But I don't see what that has to do with—"

"They had rides and a tiger and an elephant. I rode the Ferris wheel with my dad. They stopped it when we were on top. Let people off. It rocked and rocked. Freaked me out. He said it would be okay. He said we'd be fine. I climbed under his arm, and he wrapped me tight, and he said we'd be fine. He said when we got down we'd go find Mom and MeChell and we'd get some ice cream, then we'd tell them how everyone else on the Ferris wheel was screaming. Then a few years later I helped bury a dead elephant."

"Um, okay."

Clint stood up. "When are we supposed to take this time off?"

"In the next six months. Monica has a spreadsheet in the office up front."

"I'd like to start mine now." Clint took off his apron, rolled it up, set it in the chair behind him.

"You'll need to check with Monica. I'm not sure—"

Clint turned, walked out the door, through the storage room, the back door.

He stopped behind the building, lit a cigarette, tossed the filter, watched it spin in a rain puddle. Then he walked to the edge of the brush, stepping on saplings, feeling them snap to stubs until he got to the slight rise in the earth. He kneeled, dug a hole. Reached into his back pocket, pulled out the paper from the courthouse and set it in the hole, then covered it with damp dirt. He lay down in a small clearing, looked up at the vacant sky, and closed his eyes.

He's covered in a cold darkness. A sheet, slipping back against his head, his ears. Between his eyes, pressing against him, a cold metal pole. Voices around him. Stern. Yelling. He can't understand what they are saying, but knows it is important. He pushes the pole, small steps, his legs in slacking chains, scraping grit beneath him. The pole leans forward as the darkness lifts, light from under the sheet of nightfall. Forward steps, shuffling. Small. The pole heavier as it moves upright, sunlight and coolness, air slicing in. He can see the men standing around, can see some children underneath the edge of the sheet, all moving their hands together, making sharp, smacking sounds over and over. And then the lightness grows and the hand smacking stops as the voices began to warn, a scream and movement, and the empty blackness is gone and the pole is touching the sun and the power of the sun, the light fills him as the heavens descend into his body, filling him with angel radiance, the cold and darkness not even a memory and the light, the heat fills him. And for a moment he is everything and everything is him until he shatters, breaking into the sparks of heaven, drifting, falling to the earth like cigarette ash in the rain.

THE THING WITH FEATHERS

The boy sat in a folding chair at the kitchen table, a boomerang pattern in a pale sea of Formica, loading playing cards into a black plastic shuffler. Half a stack on a ledge on one side. Half on the other. Split the cards on either side of the cube, nine or ten inches each way. He looked through the kitchen window for a few seconds, then flicked the switch, the fwoosh and clicking until all the cards had been placed in a new order. He'd look at the fresh stacks, a new set of possibilities. Eight of spades on top. Jack of hearts on the bottom. Then thumb through the deck until he found the aces. Then split the cards back into two stacks, feed them through each side of the machine again. Two of clubs on the bottom. Four of spades on the top. Then he split the cards another time. His father had been gone for three days.

Averdale Tatum fumbled through the junk drawer to find her nephew a fresh set of Evereadys. She pulled one out, held it up, looking at the image of the electrocuted cat jumping through the number nine, and handed it to the boy.

"These are Cs," he said. "Need Ds."

She took the battery back, set it on the counter. Dug through a misfolded road map, a string of red ribbon, a tape measure, two

Phillips-head screwdrivers, a handful of loose, picture-hanging nails no one needed.

She shut the drawer, pulled it open again to tuck the ribbon back in. Closed it shut. "You're ten years old. Whyn't you go outside and play?" she asked. "I got some cleaning up to do."

The boy held the barrel of his Daisy pellet gun, dragging the butt along the dirt and gravel road toward the cutoff for the oil well. Cans. Bottles. Line 'em up and knock 'em down. He held the barrel of the gun at the end, swung the rifle like a golf club, sweeping chunks of rock from one side of the road to the other.

The white clouds blew like lace across the pale blue sky. Just before he got to the turn, he saw a chicken hawk on the wires above him, at the edge of the clear-cut field. The boy held the rifle in the fold of his arm, reached into his pocket for the white, plastic box, slid a handful of pellets into the butt of the gun, twisted closed the opening. He lifted the rifle, set the sights at the bird's back. He took a deep breath, and when he'd finished the exhale, he pulled the trigger, heard the spit of air as the pellet flew toward the bird. The bird stayed still, and the boy pulled the trigger again. And again, stepping forward.

Averdale Tatum went through the mail she'd taken from her brother's house that morning. Important Information Enclosed. Reply Today. Sign Up and Save. She pulled the only bill from the stack, slid the rest into the kitchen garbage.

Standing at the refrigerator door, she pulled off a photograph of Champion Tatum and his son, standing on the church steps in Easter shirts and ties. "I have to pay your damn electric bill and watch the boy? Might as well just have the damn current shut off."

She sat down in the chair, still holding the picture. "I don't mind watching the boy," she said. "Just wish I knew when you were coming home. If you were coming home."

She looked at the picture, creased the picture in half, folded the boy away so she was just talking to her brother. "I know she shouldn't have just left the two of you like that, but people got problems, Champ. Ain't nothing you can do to hold them. You just gotta listen."

She tossed the photograph onto the table with the electric bill, the card shuffler, the mismatched salt and pepper shakers. "Did you listen?"

Then she shook her head, walked over to the window on the east side of the house, looked out at the little shed where she and her baby brother would head out for blocks of frozen peas, frost-fuzzed and stacked on wire shelves in the rusted icebox. She thought of the time they had walked in and looked up to rafters dripping with milk snakes, all red and yellow and black, swinging above them along the bicycle tires and broken chairs. She had left Champion on the cinderblock steps, eased across the floor planks, and come back with a rock-hard bag of purple hull peas held above her head.

"I shoulda done better by you, Champ," she said. "I shoulda looked after you after Eleanor did that to herself. I shoulda made you tell me where you were going, what you were up to, running off like that." She lifted her arm, wiped her nose on the shoulder of her housecoat. "Who am I talking to?" she asked out loud.

The boy walked over to where the bird had fallen, lying in a heap of briars and broken limbs. He watched the bird for a moment, waiting for it to try to fly away, but it didn't move. The boy used the barrel of his rifle to turn the bird onto its back, looking into its eyes. Deep black marbles that shone like a coffin.

When the bird blinked, the boy fell backward, but got up and walked back over to the bird. The bird twisted its neck at an angle, the way you'd ask someone "Why?" The boy wondered if maybe the bird had broken its neck.

He waited for something to happen. The bird would fly away. Maybe the bird would flap its wings and fly at his face. Maybe he'd wait long enough and the bird would die. But then what? The boy wondered what would happen, what he should do. Should he bury the bird? Say a prayer? He'd been too young last year to go to his mother's funeral, but people had come to the house after and patted him on the head. Aunt Averdale. Uncle Horace. Aunt Janeva. Cousins he'd never seen before or since. People from the church they went to on holidays. Patted him on the back. Patted him on the knee.

The boy leaned his rifle against a fence post, lay down next to the bird, and put his palm on the bird's chest. The bird fluttered at his touch, shifted along the ground, then settled under the boy's hand.

The sun was dropping behind the scrub pines, and the boy had to close his eyes to the glare. He thought of lying in bed with his mother when she got the sadness. Of her stroking his hair and mumbling a song to him until they both fell asleep. So he hummed a little to the bird, then started singing the only thing he could think of to sing. The song he heard at the end of every service, waiting to see if someone had been saved. Every head bowed. Every eye closed. "Just as I am, without one plea. But that thy blood was shed for me." He hummed some more, working in words when he could remember them. "With many a conflict, many a doubt. Oh, Lamb of God."

He kept his eyes closed as he hummed, took slow breaths. He thought about the story of Peter cutting off the Roman soldier's ear and Jesus putting the man's ear back. He thought of his Sunday school teacher walking him down to the church office where his father met him, everyone else crying. The news that his mother was gone. That she wouldn't wake up. All the people in the church office standing around, with his father in the chair. So many men in suits and ushers' boutonnieres, ready to go in to the church service. To big church. But now standing in the church office with his father sitting in a chair and some women in flowery dresses handing each other Kleenex. And him standing in the doorway with his Sunday school teacher, Miss Velma, until one of the women looked and saw him and ran over at him and scooped him up and hugged him and said she was sorry and everything was going to be all right and it would be fine and it would be okay. It's bad now, but will be okay. It will be okay. But it wasn't.

Averdale Tatum pulled the mason jars from the box, set them one at a time into the sink, turned on the tap, set a box of pectin on the counter. She pulled jar tongs from the drawer, pulled her apron from the back of the door. She'd always set aside extra jars of jellies and pickles for Champion. Sweet pickles for the boy, the kind he called "bug pickles" because of the black spice balls floating around the jar like bug eggs.

He'd be back the end of the week, Champion had told her, but she didn't believe him. She'd seen him drifting away from Eleanor for a couple of years, like he always had. A little nudge this way or that. Inertia. The sort of thing where someone says, "Let's do this" and you just go along. When they were growing up, mostly left to themselves, she hadn't minded so much. Let's go see what the creek washed up. Let's play school at the old barn. When Champion had started dating Eleanor, Averdale had noticed a new spark to him. A sparkle. Trying new things. Out on the town. Raising a family. But then he and the boy had started coming to

Sunday dinners without her. And Averdale got the feeling that maybe Champion was sitting on the side of the creek, watching Eleanor drift along. And then when she—when she left like that—Averdale realized the sparkle she'd seen had just been someone else's reflection. That Champion was just the boy standing back on the cinderblock steps, waiting.

She looked through the kitchen window to see her nephew walking across the yard, dragging his pellet gun in one hand, holding a bird cradled in his other arm.

Outside the house, she looked at the bird, pulled it loose from the boy. Then she held the boy's shoulders tight in her hands.

"What did you do?" she asked. Then she looked at the bird, the rifle.

"Shot it. I didn't mean to kill it," he said. "I just shot it. We gotta get it some help. We gotta get it to the hospital."

She squeezed the boy tight, wiped her nose on her shoulder. Took a deep breath. "Let it go," she said.

The boy sniffled, pulled away, rubbed his nose on the back of his wrist. "But," he stammered.

"Ain't nothing we can do. Let it go," Averdale Tatum said again, turning him toward the house. "Once a thing starts going, can't nothing bring it back."

GOOD MONEY

In the photograph I'm holding my grandfather's baseball glove.

Short. Stubby. An early glove, back before Spittin' Bill Doak of the St. Louis Cardinals made them put in the webbing. A glove. Not a mitt. Old when my grandfather had it.

Doak retired to Florida and opened a candy shop. He died in November of 1954. The next year my grandfather was on his way home from work when he was shot in the back six times and died in a ditch alongside Highway 29, two miles south of Bradley, Arkansas. They never found his truck.

I was pulling pictures from boxes when my grandmother walked into the room.

"Find anything worth keeping?" she asked.

I said I'd found a few things, nodded toward a toppled stack of pictures and books. A journal. A pocket watch. A box of cufflinks and tiepins. A silver dollar.

She picked up the silver dollar, turned it around in her hand. "This here is a Peace Dollar."

I had no idea.

"The artist modeled Lady Liberty after his own wife. Take a gander. 1934." She handed the coin back to me. "Your grandfather got that from a man over in El Dorado for something. Can't remember now. Called it his lucky coin."

"You want it?" I asked.

"No, no. You need the luck more than I do." She winked. "See the woman? Lady Liberty? Everyone got all hot and bothered because the woman has her mouth open."

I looked at the coin. "What's wrong with that?"

"Nothing," she said, "now." Then she laughed a little high-pitched cough. "You going through your mama's stuff today? Your daddy's?"

"I don't think so," I said. "Got a job interview at three."

She hummed a little in agreement. "Want something to eat before you go? Leftover chicken. Rustle you up some pie, I imagine."

✢ ✢ ✢

I was standing at the sink, looking out the window and washing out my glass.

My grandmother squeaked back in her chair. "What's this job? This the one your cousin Cleovis set you up with?"

"No, that one didn't work out. This one is with a guy down on Dorcheat."

"On Dorcheat Bayou?" She whistled through her dentures. "Roy, hadn't been nothing doing down there since a hundred years ago." She laughed.

"Yeah. I know. He wants to start up some canoe business. Said he does some fishing down there now. A little trapping. Local meat and fish for these restaurants around."

She shook her head. "I can't see it," she said. "But I never did have a head for business. That was your Pawpaw's thing, you know." She reached across the green-and-white checked, vinyl tablecloth, pulled along the photograph of me with the baseball glove. "Yes, sir. He knew how to take care of us. Yes, sir, he did."

She stood up from the table and I looked back out the window as she re-snapped the middle of her housecoat.

I pulled a butterscotch candy from a bowl on the television, kissed her goodbye, and headed to the cabin on Dorcheat.

In thirty minutes, I was listening to a man I'd never met explain how I could make good money by killing his wife next Wednesday night during choir practice.

That Wednesday night, the man pulled out of his driveway and flashed his lights as he passed my car. When I reached the house, I took the hidden key from under the flowerpot and let myself into the mudroom.

I pulled the pistol from my jacket pocket. She was folding clothes in the guest room. A stack of white towels was on the bed. Soft. Warm. Clean.

She screamed when I put the gun to the side of her head and clamped my left hand across her mouth.

I showed her the gun and nodded. Then I put my finger to my lips. Shhh. She nodded back and I took my other hand away.

She tried to ask me not to hurt her, but she was shaking too much, her jaw in some sort of seizure.

I pushed the towels to the side of the bed and the stack toppled over. Then I lowered her to a sitting position and stood in front of her.

On the wall behind the bed was a shelf full of trophies. Little silver baseball players standing on top of columns and blocks. A team photograph, decades old, of little boys in bright yellow shirts standing in a field.

The television in the corner was muted. Onscreen police scientists in lab coats pretended to look at things in microscopes.

Making everything better after a murder. Catching killers. Keeping people safe.

I pointed the gun between the woman's eyes until she closed them. Then I found a chair along the wall. I reached back and pulled it forward. I sat down in the chair and tried to explain the situation to her.

"He knows?" she asked.

"Yeah."

"How much?"

"Enough."

"Does he know that James and I are in love? That I'm going to divorce him?"

"I imagine so," I said. "Pretty much why he came up with tonight's solution."

"Why you? Is this what you do? Rape people? Kill people?"

"Friend of a friend had a job."

"So what now?" she asked.

"Up to you," I said.

She nodded. "What am I worth, if I can ask?"

"The job, you mean?"

She nodded, and I told her three thousand. Her husband and I had settled on eight hundred, but she seemed nice and I didn't want her to feel cheap.

"Did he pay you? Good money?"

I shook my head, trying to think what would sound real. "Wanted to make sure this was done right. Owes me half."

She nodded again and asked if she could stand up. She walked to the closet, pulled out a footstool, and stepped up. From behind a stack of sweaters she pulled a small box. She opened it and counted out some money. "That's all I have. It's what he owes you. Plus."

"You sure?" I asked.

"I'm sure," she said, putting the box back. "I have a feeling money won't be a problem soon."

On the way out I wiped away my fingerprints, put the key back under the flowerpot. Walking back to my car, I slid the pistol back into my jacket. Then I folded the money she'd given me into the wad I'd gotten from him.

+ + +

The next night I took my grandmother out to eat at Wiley's on the Bayou. Catfish. Hush puppies. I wanted to ask her about my grandfather's journal, about whether she'd read it after he died. About whether she knew he met a woman after work during his last year.

She pulled a clump of fish bones from her mouth, lined them up in a neat row along the edge of the plate. Dipped a hush puppy in ketchup. "Isn't this a nice night?" she asked, looking out the window, through the cypress trees in the bayou. Watching the sun go yellow and red in the distance.

"Yes, ma'am." I took the last sip of my tea, rattled the cup down so the waitress could hear. "I had a question for you about Pawpaw."

"Yes, sir. The world is full of questions." She moved her chair back from the table just a little bit. "Like how you came to be able to afford taking your old grandmother out on a date."

I put my hand into my front pocket, rubbed my grandfather's lucky coin. The waitress made it back, filled me up with sweet tea, and went away. The ceiling fan thunked around above us, out of rhythm but still working.

My grandmother folded her hands into her lap. "But you had a question first. About your grandfather."

I took a sip of tea, folded the napkin to a clean spot, and wiped my mouth. Then I looked at the sunset and asked a different question.

ALL STAR

"They want me to play short," he said, running across the field to the chainlink fence where Nancy and I were standing by the dugout.

I asked him to tell me again.

"Yeah, Coach said they wanted to see me play short, 'cause they already got two catchers."

"Who's got two catchers? Slow down. Who's got two catchers?"

"The All-Star team. Said he wants me to play short. Show them I can play. Said I had a shot at making the All-Star team."

I said it was great, even though I wasn't so sure.

"Coach said I need my glove. To play the field."

"You didn't bring your other glove?"

He looked down at the weeds growing through the bottom of the fence. "No, sir."

"Why not?" I asked, maybe a little rough. Nancy squeezed my elbow.

"Sorry, Dad. I just, I just didn't think I'd need it. Ain't used it all year."

Nancy cleared her throat. "Haven't used it all year."

"Sorry."

I took a slow breath. "Where is it?" I asked, not moving my jaw.

"In my bedroom."

"Any idea exactly *where* in your bedroom?"

"I don't, I mean, maybe, I don't know."

Nancy squeezed my arm again. "Maybe in your closet, sweetie? Maybe on your shelf? Maybe that's where you left it last time?"

"Yes, ma'am. That's right. On the shelf with all my Hot Wheels. It's there."

"All right," I said, and he ran back onto the field with his catcher's mitt.

"Back as quick as I can."

"If he makes the All-Star team," Nancy started. "I mean, that's great, but . . . "

"You mean the travel?"

"Right. It gets, you know, expensive traveling. Then if they get out of regionals . . . "

"I know," I said, kissing her on the forehead. "One thing at a time. We'll figure it out." Behind her, the boy was walking around the infield, kicking stones clear.

"We can't afford to . . . "

"It's fine. We'll figure it out."

"That's what you always say."

"I do?"

She grinned. "Yeah."

"Back in a bit."

"Hey," she said, running after me, leaning toward my face and whispering, "you paid the credit card?"

"Which one?"

"The JanFed one."

"Yeah."

"Okay." She kissed me and walked back to the fence.

I passed Dougie Robinson on the way to my truck. "Giving up already? No faith in the Whispering Pines Tigers?"

"What's going on, Dougie? Your boy playing today?"

"Yeah. Pitching. Coach says he's the next Skinny Dennis McWilliams. How about yours?"

"Yeah," I said. "Got him playing short."

"Short? What's that about?"

"Something the coach is doing, I guess. Heading home to get the right glove."

"Maybe you could get one from Whispering Pines?"

"How you mean?"

"Like Hank over at the Mini-Mart. He sponsors the team, so the kids all get Icees and candy bars after the game. Figure since Whispering Pines sponsors you guys, maybe the nursing home can give you some gloves. You know, latex or whatever. Like it would matter." Dougie elbowed the guy next to him, and they both laughed.

"I'll bring it up, Dougie. Thanks."

"Hey, how's the job hunt going?" I heard him ask as I walked away.

The glove was on the shelf, like the boy had said, next to a few cars, a couple of comics, and a blue and gold baseball cap. The year before for his birthday, all he'd asked for was a baseball cap. Light blue with gold stars. "Like the All-Stars have," he said. So I went down to the athletic supply store by Piggly Wiggly and got him this cap and a brand-new baseball. They wouldn't let me have one of the All-Star caps they made for the team, which makes sense, I guess.

He had opened the box and spent the afternoon bending the cap's bill, trying it on. Bending the bill again. Finding a marker, writing his name on the underside of the bill. Then writing his number next to it. If he made the team, we'd have to get him a real cap. And a real jersey, too. And then all the travel. Sixty bucks for motels. Twenty for meals. If we were careful, maybe we could make some room on one of the cards. After the game, I could call and see about increasing the limit on one of them. Maybe we had something we could sell online. Maybe I'd start buying an extra lottery ticket each Monday. We'd figure it out.

I drove by the ATM to see whether Nancy's paycheck had maybe gone in early, but it hadn't. I took the envelope with our JanFed payment from behind the sun visor, slid it into the glove box. I'd check the balance again on Monday.

He was in the dugout when I got back, waiting for his chance to bat, which usually didn't come until the third inning. I bent the fence back a little by the wall of the dugout, slid his glove through. The huge, floppy piece of leather he'd talked his grandmother into getting him at Western Auto. An outfielder's glove, probably made for softball. He'd convinced her that a bigger glove was better, and since this was the biggest, it had to be the best. It was money we didn't have, so what can you say? You say "thank you" is what you say.

They took the field and the Robinson kid on the Rebel Mini-Mart Marlins sent the first pitch over the broken scoreboard, then trotted his home-run walk like I'm sure his daddy taught him. I looked across the field and saw Dougie standing on the bleachers, arms raised. He saw me looking at him, made a gun with his fingers, then shot me. Pulled his index finger back, blew off the imaginary smoke.

A kid called Caleb flied out to the salvage yard sign in left. The next batter started the trouble, lining one to my boy, who got caught on an in-between hop but managed to knock the ball down, then throw the ball to the coach's kid at first about five seconds too late.

I wanted the coach to call "Time," to waddle his ass out to the mound and make sure my boy knew who was covering second, who would take the throw on a steal. But he didn't. He sat on the bench in the dugout, working a pencil up and down a clipboard, spitting sunflower seeds onto the ground while my son stood alone in the field, adjusting his cap.

Nancy rubbed my shoulder. "You all right?"

"Yeah. Just into the game, I guess."

"Don't worry. He'll do fine," she said.

"That's what you always say."

She kissed my shoulder, patted the top of my knee. "Just relax."

The next kid hit a foul ball over the dugout, into the open area where the kids were playing cupball by wadding up a Coke cup, using it for a ball, an open palm for a bat. They chased after the foul ball. One of the kids grabbed it and walked up to the concession stand for a free sno-cone.

"He makes the team, it'll be fine, right? Maybe he makes the high school team. College scholarship."

"Sure."

"Just think of what he could do with a college education," Nancy said.

"Honey, he's twelve."

"I know. But you have to plan ahead. We have to start thinking about these things. Putting some money away."

The Marlins at bat, one of the Lacewell bunch, let a couple go by him to fill the count.

"Honey, calm down," Nancy said. "You're going to have another heart attack."

"I'm fine," I said. "Just want the boy to do well." One play might do it. A spinning catch. A strong throw. Starting the double play. When the boy sat down at the breakfast table and his pants rode up above his socks, I'd joked that we were one growth spurt away from declaring bankruptcy.

"Me, too," Nancy said. "He'll be fine."

Then the Lacewell kid hit a slow roller to short, which my boy charged, picked up barehanded as the runner made it to second and the batter had a few steps to go. My boy cocked his elbow, snapping his throw like an All-Star, and the whole town watched the ball sail two feet wide of the fat coach's fat kid.

THAT KIND
OF FACE

The old man was holding the framed photograph, turning it around in his hand, pointing to the men one at a time. Around a desk. Men in polyester dress shirts. Thick, loose ties. Shoulder holsters.

"Wojo, I can't remember the guy's name. Real nice guy. The Asian guy, he was a funny little fella. And the black guy and the Jew. They were class acts, every one of them. You probably don't even remember *Barney Miller*, do you?"

"Yeah, I remember the show," Roy said, looking at the other pictures the man had on the wall.

The old man turned the volume back up on the ball game. Houston was up by a run over the Cardinals. Then journeyman reliever Johnny White gave up a walk to load the bases.

"Max Gail," the old man said, slapping his hands together. "Wojo. The guy's name was Max Gail. The actor."

"Okay," Roy said.

The old man shut the game off when a wild pitch tied the game. He turned to Roy, still standing at the wall of pictures. "That's me even younger with the *Adam-12* crew. Named my boys after those two. Pete Malloy and Jim Reed. Good guys."

Roy thought about the man's two boys, men when they were killed in Iraq. He wondered whether Father's Day was any worse than the rest of them. If the old man missed them so much every day that holidays couldn't be any worse. The way Roy missed his parents all year, every year for the past decade, Mother's Day and Father's Day didn't matter too much. Like tossing a match into a burned-out car.

"So you used to be an actor? Like a long time ago?"

"Not that long ago," the old man said. "I was the guy they'd pick up in the first part of the show, then find out—whatever it was—I didn't do it." The man took a drink from his cup, then set it back on the table next to him. "A good suspect, they said. That kind of face."

The men sat in silence, watching the white dot on the TV screen fade away.

"I wanted to ask you about the Darby money," Roy said. "Bonnie and Clyde."

"Bonnie and Clyde?" The old man laughed. "No, they were dead before I was born. I'm not that old. Killed in Louisiana by a group of Texas cops. Chased all over the South, robbing and killing. Frank Hamer finally got those bastards, though. You know, you hear all the damn time about Pat Garrett and what a hero he was for tracking down Billy the Kid. Nobody remembers Hamer. But they got shrines to Bonnie and Clyde. Nobody gives two shits for Hamer, for the good guys. Not two shits."

"What about Darby?" Roy asked, working the old man back on the subject.

"H. D. Darby," the old man said. "They grabbed him and a girl down around Ruston and dumped them over in Waldo. Don't remember the girl's name."

"Waldo?"

"Yeah, Waldo," the old man said. "Not ten miles from where you're sitting. Bonnie and Clyde dropped the pair off there. And you want to know something scary?"

Roy said he did.

"Bonnie Parker asked Mr. Darby what he did for a living. And you know what he told her?"

He didn't.

"He told her he was an undertaker."

"Undertaker?"

"Right." The old man tapped his nose. "When he told her that, when he says that to her, Miss Bonnie Parker laughed and laughed and said that maybe someday soon Mr. Darby would work on her."

"Okay."

The old man took another drink. Set the glass down. "Soon enough Bonnie and Clyde were shot dead in Louisiana and Mr. Darby was one of the undertakers who worked on them."

They talked a few more minutes about Bonnie and Clyde. Then Roy asked about the hideout.

"Old farmhouse between Magnolia and Waldo. Nobody's real sure where. Three oak trees form a triangle. In the middle they buried a chest. That's all folks know for sure. Lot of treasure hunters turned over a lot of Columbia County dirt back in the '30s and '40s looking for it, but no one ever found anything."

"Still there?"

"Nobody ever claimed it," the old man said.

"So what do you think?" Roy asked. "Worth looking for?"

"That why you're asking?"

"Just saw a documentary about it. Got to thinking about it, that's all."

The old man twisted around, trying to pop his neck. He gave up. Took another drink. "You know who Myrna Loy is?"

"From *The Thin Man* movies?"

"Yeah, sure. That's what everyone remembers her for. *The Thin Man.*" He smacked his lips together for a bit. "Ever see *Across the Pacific? The Desert Song?*"

Roy said he hadn't.

"Jesus God." The old man shook his head. "What a woman."

Roy waited, then, "Not sure what this has to do with Bonnie and Clyde."

"You were asking if it was worth it. I went to Hollywood back in the '60s, looking for Myrna Loy. She was a little older than I was. She was probably, hell, fifty or sixty then. Saw a show on the TV the other day about that. Older women and younger men. They've got a name for that now. Can't remember what it is. But we didn't have shows like that back then. We had Mike Douglas and Andy Griffith. You probably don't remember them either, but they were something special. They don't make them like that anymore."

"Okay."

"So I go there looking for Miss Loy. You know she had four husbands? Divorced all four of them. What I'm going the long way around the barn to tell you is you go searching for something and you don't know what you're going to find. I go searching for Miss Loy and meet my Abigail Landry and we have two great boys and a great life. Luckiest man alive." He leaned his head back on the recliner, looked off at something. "You go out looking for something, maybe there's something looking for you. Maybe you need to let it find you."

"Somebody goes looking for the Bonnie and Clyde money, maybe they find it, maybe they find a lot of dirt."

"I don't know what I'm talking about, Roy. Just looking at all these old pictures. You get old enough, you're looking back at whoever you were and wondering how much of that person is left."

"You ever find Myrna Loy?"

"I oughta tell you I met her and she was fat and ugly. Keep you from chasing after nonsense."

"You never saw her?"

"No, just in the movies." The old man found the remote on the side table, turned on some baseball highlights, then muted the TV. "Roy, you remember what I told you the first day I saw you? After you moved in with your grandma?"

"You said if I leave grass clippings on your carport you'll skin me alive."

The old man laughed. "I said you look like your grandpa."

"Yeah, well. I guess I ought to."

"Not that much. You know, you get pieces from everybody. But you got most of your pieces from him. He was a good man, your grandpa."

"So I'm told."

"And I'm guessing you were told your grandpa went looking for that money, too."

Roy looked away.

"Your grandma tell you that? That where you got that?"

"Just going through some old boxes of stuff at her house is all. Got me thinking."

"Got him thinking, too. Fool's gold, Roy. Myrna Loy. Bonnie and Clyde treasure. Being a hero for your country. Damn it, you'd best just cut your grass and keep your head down, son. Stop hoping after something that ain't there."

"Worked out for you, though."

The old man nodded. "Ask your grandpa how it worked out for him."

The old man turned the game back on, poured himself another drink, then fell asleep before the ice had melted.

Roy stood at the wall, looking at the photographs. Cop shows from the '60s and '70s. Autographs from cast members. Notes they wrote the old man on the edges of the pictures. The shows that were canceled. The stars who made it. Those who didn't. He looked into the faces, the eyes of each person, trying to find something that stood out. That kind of face. Something in the eyes, a reflection, a longing.

Roy picked up the picture cube from the top of the television. One of the old man's sons in a Little League uniform. Another, about two or three years old, putting Easter eggs into a basket. One picture of the two boys together in their late teens wearing desert fatigues, leaning against a light brown tank with the words "Miss You, Pop" ink-smeared on the edge.

Roy rolled the cube around in his hands, trying to fill it with pictures of the family he didn't have. He reached into his back pocket, took out his bandana, wiped the dust from the top of the television, and set the cube back down.

"Happy Father's Day," Roy whispered as he slid the glass door shut and walked back to his truck.

ON ACCOUNT

Hurley's truck wasn't there when I pulled up, so I went around back of the place to look at the boat.

I had a good enough setup to just tow the fucker right off if I wanted to, but that ain't what I was set for. I went and knocked on the screen door in back. Shaky cinderblock steps next to a half-finished deck. Budweiser cans, stomped and squashed, spread around the yard like some drunk midgets had been playing a hop-scotch game last night before the storm.

Hurley's girlfriend answered. Agreeable gal. V-neck T-shirt. Can of Bud. Nice, smooth tan. Not much else. She made a point of showing me she was cold. Couple points, I figure.

"You Cleovis? You here for the boat?"

I explained as how I was.

She wanted me to come in and she'd get the keys to the trailer lock. No sense making a big mess of shit, she said.

I came in and sat down at their kitchen table. A card table. Duct tape not quite covering up a cut at the edge. Three chairs. Unmatched.

She hollered from across the hall. "Can I talk you out of taking the boat just yet?"

I said Bill had been pretty clear about how I was supposed to conduct things with her no-account boyfriend. He'd suggested that I bring back the fucking boat and stop fucking around or he'd fucking shove a fucking ramrod up my fucking ass. I kinda gave her the short version.

She came out into the kitchen. She'd taken off the T-shirt. I couldn't see any tan lines from where I was, so I took a closer look.

After we finished, she brought me a can of beer and lay back down on the bed, resting on her elbows.

"So maybe you come back for the boat next week?"

I said I wasn't so sure about that.

She rolled over on her back and looked up at me. "See, Hurley's got this job and he's good for it. I mean, I'm kinda looking out for him, you know? Making sure shit gets took care of. That's how come I'm offering this little payment to you, you know. Kinda on account."

I didn't say anything. I thought about her asshole boyfriend. His worthless self.

"You know, on account of Hurley not being good for much. I gotta take care of things."

I stopped thinking about her boyfriend when she put her hand between my legs and took care of things. Again.

When we were done that time, I got up and said I'd see about giving them a little more time. I said "an extension," and she giggled.

I drove back up the hill and stopped at the church parking lot. Pulled up next to Hurley's truck.

"Shit, Cleovis. Took you long enough," he said.

I said it sure did and that he had another few days to get the money to Bill. If not, I'd have to come back.

"I can't lose that boat," he said. "She's the love of my life."

I drove off. On account of not wanting to have to shoot him before I saw his girlfriend again.

SMOKE FADES AWAY

My bootlace got hung up on barbed wire, and the loop unraveled.
I stepped up onto a fallen post, looked across the field to the dark
cabin on the edge of the woods. Lights on inside. A cobweb trail of
smoke fading away above. The orange sunlight turning pink along
the line of scrub pine. Another two hundred yards and I'd be there.

The weeds were beaten down pretty good through the field.
Of course, most of this area was after half the county spent the
week searching for Staci McMahen. I took a breath in the cool-
ing dusk, prayed I'd have better luck finding this fucking dog.
Whatever luck I had left since the killings at La Vega. The bomb
in Bucaramanga.

I saw movement under the porch. Dogs. Coons. Skunks. Hell
if I could tell from here. I got closer and saw two people moving around the front room, shirtless white men with beer guts
bouncing over opened jeans, the hollow thunks from the wooden
floorboards beating time to muffled screams that came and went
like smoke in the wind.

I squatted down at the porch, looked under the house for dog
eyes. Chunks of glass. Part of a lawn mower. Ice chest. Then I felt
something sting my neck. The point of a buck knife.

I put my hands on the edge of the porch and stood up slowly. I heard another scream from inside the house. Louder this time. High-pitched. A screech. Then a gurgling, as though the voice couldn't contain the violence.

When the guy with the knife flinched, I pulled away and swept his legs. Then I grabbed his knife hand and used the hilt to pop his temple, knock him out. Took two tries, but he stayed down.

I tossed the knife under the porch, walked around the side of the house, and stood out of the glow, looking into the window. Two more shirtless men, sitting around, smoking cigars and drinking beer from cans. A TV strobing against the walls, the laughing faces. Some I knew. The guy who runs the tire place on the way to Magnolia. One of the Sawyer boys. The Pribble boy from the box store.

The next room back I saw her. Found a five-gallon bucket to get a better look, leaning up to the window. Even in the dim light, under a swollen face and blood-caked hair spread against the table, I knew Staci McMahen.

I start counting the guys in the house by room. One out front. Two. Another two.

I walked up the three wood-plank steps in the back, pulled open the screen door, and stepped into the mudroom. No one looked up, and I figured there'd been a good deal of traffic coming through. I looked into the far room, past a couple shaking, naked men waiting in line, to see the guy from out front come in, screaming all kinds of hell. The houseful looked around, grabbing pants and shirts. Then a couple of them saw me. One of the guys near Staci pulled a pistol from a side table and raised it at me. Asked me the fuck I think I'm doing.

"Looking for a dog."

He wanted to know the fuck that's supposed to mean.

Someone said something about the peckerwood having a smart mouth. Someone said something about teaching the boy some fucking manners.

Then the Sawyer boy stepped into the room from a side door. Said he knows me. "Got a medal, dincha? Some Brazilian bullshit, right? Real fancy hero, fellas. This here's Dougie Robinson's little brother. Let's let this little fucker feel at home."

"Colombia," I said. "La Ciudad Bonita de Colombia."

The fuck you talking foreign for, he wanted to know. Took a step toward me. I moved to him, kept his gun hand down while I put my forehead into his nose. The house rattled a stampede as I turned him, catching a slug in his back. I heard thunder as the house wanted to rip apart, men falling out the front door, men coming toward me. He tried to pull away, hand to his nose, until I let him take his gun out, then snapped his wrist and sent a bullet under his jaw, through the top of his skull. The heat and powder from the shot stung my eyes, and I was looking through tears as the Pribble boy and someone I didn't know started to swing for me.

I dropped to the floor, flicked open the razor from my boot, and came up across their faces in a tight arc, sending them falling back, one through the window, one deeper into the house. He was crawling back by the time I got to him, steel toe in the balls. He embryoed up, and I was on him with the razor before he made a sound. I was taking too long, thinking about what they'd done, and the Pribble boy who'd gone through the window was back in the house, coming into the room. He tossed the five-gallon bucket at my head. I twisted the razor in my hand, and gashed him from belly to beard as he reached across his bloody gut like he was trying to keep his coat closed in the rain.

Aside from the dead, the dying, it was just me and Staci in the house. I walked from room to room to make sure, seeing the moonlit dust settle in the front yard.

I looked at Staci, ran my fingers along the table, worked through the blood and juices to find where the rope stopped and her arm began. I slit one rope loose and she looked up at me, shaking. She tried to say "thank you" but nothing came out.

I thought about taking her out of there. Holding her in my arms across the field, like carrying out the wounded near La Vega to the trucks, sorting the breathing from the corpses. The wounded you hold, chest tight in a flatbed truck under a star-pricked sky to a safe house in Rosas. Handing over a child filled with horror, handing over an eternal burden. The family unable to move on. To grieve. A wound that never heals. A corpse you can never bury. Handing them back a fragment. The ones left charred, falling apart like last night's firewood. The light behind their eyes burned into graying ash as the smoke fades away.

I moved to the Sawyer boy's body, rolled him until I found the pistol, then popped a red dot through Staci's forehead.

I turned back to hear scratching on the screen door. A few dogs looking for help. I wiped the gun, put it back in Sawyer's hand, then set some curtains on fire.

I moved down the back steps, picking up the terrier and putting him in my jacket. Started the long walk home.

RECEPTION

My Aunt Velma wiped the Red Man juice from her chin, put the coffee can back on the TV tray. "Doyle, you just need to get yourself down there and fix her antenna is what you need to do."

"I will, Aunt Vee, I will. Just gotta finish this up first," I said. I pulled my cap up, sleeved off the sweat from my head.

I'd been staying with my aunt off and on for the past year, ever since I'd gotten laid off from the flooring place outside Magnolia. Price of gas these days, wasn't worth it anyway. I'd finished a line of caulking on the inside of the leaky window and was cleaning it up with the edge of one of those credit cards they send you in the mail. Sign up and spend $5,000 and I'd get 5,000 points to take the family to Disney World. I don't have a family.

So I dragged the edge of the card along the window frame, worked the caulking into the corners as best I could, then used a rag to wipe off all the excess. I wiped the card off on the same rag, then slid the card into my pocket where I used to keep a wallet. "She say what was wrong with it?"

"Said it was broke. I don't need her and her niece coming up here every damned day to watch my stories with me and eat up all my goddamned food. I swear I've never seen a girl put away so many gizzards in one sitting."

Her stories. *As the World Turns. Guiding Light.* Her stories. Her world. When I started staying here, she'd send me out on errands in the early afternoon so I wouldn't get in her way. Most days I didn't have anywhere else to go, so I'd just walk up and down the road picking up cans out of the ditches. Down to Mr. Tatum's place and then back again was pretty close to long enough for me to stay away. Usually managed enough cans to make it worthwhile, too. After a while I'd stay and keep my mouth shut. Little while after that, I'd say something about one of the characters. One day I said Blake Thorpe looks like Miss Angela down at the Texaco. Turns out my aunt doesn't much care for Miss Angela. I didn't say too much after that.

"I'll see what I can do," I said, using a loose nail from the windowsill to clean some of the caulk from under my thumbnail, "but I'm not much of an electrician."

"Weren't much of a plank layer before that, were you?"

"They cut me back. Wasn't my fault the housing market went to hell."

She wiped a little more Red Man from her chin. "You watch your mouth, young man."

"Yes, ma'am."

"Guess it wasn't your fault Ellie walked out on you, was it?"

I sent the tip of the nail into my thumb, coughed. "No, ma'am."

"Right. Right. What's she doing now? Who's she staying with?"

"I don't know."

"I heard somebody down at the beauty shop say they saw her with that Dwayne boy used to go around with MeChell from the insurance place. Robert's youngest."

"I wouldn't know. I don't see her that much."

"Yeah, well, whose fault is that?"

I don't know how it went so wrong with Ellie. I should have done things differently, I guess. I just never knew which things. I walked to the back of the house to the couch where my pillow and radio were and scanned for any afternoon baseball games. On a good day, sometimes I could get a Texas Rangers game. I didn't much care for any of them, but if they were playing the New York Yankees, at least I'd have someone to root against. Sometimes it just works out better to root against something.

The weather was pretty clear, which isn't always the best for picking up games on the radio. But after the weather we'd had, I'd take clear and quiet. Last week we had some awful storms come through. Took out a church up near Emerson and a couple of old farmhouses. Flooded most of the back roads around here. And other smaller problems. Like the antenna on Miss Imogene Crawford's place.

Aunt Vee screamed from the front of the house. I could picture her leaning up on the arms of the chair, taking a deep breath. "How's about you fix that woman's antenna right and that'll be your rent check for the month? Think you can manage that?"

So I took a couple of screwdrivers, a pair of pliers, a ball-peen hammer, and half a roll of duct tape, dropped them in a green pillowcase, and headed down to Miss Imogene's house.

By the time I got down to her place, I had sweat and grit on the back of my neck. I knocked at her door, and she let me in. She offered me a glass of water, and I sat down in the living room. Thick red and brown shag carpeting matched most of the furniture and made the couch look like a little hill in the floor. I sat down and she brought me a glass of warm tap water and I downed it in a couple of swallows.

I started to tell her why I was there when she walked over to the television set and turned it off. I hadn't even noticed the thing had been on. You get that way sometimes. You get something in your head that you have to do and you get focused on it so strong that you forget what you set out to do. You can get that way laying floors. You get so caught up in going one direction, then you look up and you're caught in a corner and everything's gone off kilter by a quarter inch.

"Doyle, you know you don't need an excuse to stop by, but I see you got a pillowcase full of something there."

I looked down at the tools and felt like I'd just dragged a mess of wet squirrels into her house. "Aunt Vee said maybe you could use some help down here on your antenna," I said because those were the words I'd practiced on the way down and I hadn't had time to think of anything else.

She looked puzzled, turned her head like my Aunt Vee did whenever something really weird would happen. Like if someone would say, "Today, the part of Alan-Michael Spaulding will be played by seventeen flaming armadillos."

But then her niece started hollering from the back of the house somewhere. "I'm still hungry. I'm still hungry. I'm still hungry." A chant almost, and she took that last "hungry" and let it linger out there like "hoooongree" in some weird monster kind of rumbling. Then she was asking why can't they ever have anything to eat and she knows it costs money and why can't they ever get any money. She was walking and talking and by then she'd come to the end of the hall and could see that I was sitting there with a pillowcase between my feet.

I started looking anywhere else. Over to the photographs on the fireplace mantle. Over to the shelves where Miss Imogene had all her collectible dolls. Shelves that were empty now except for the doll stands and the ghosting dust around the edges.

So Miss Imogene sat there for a second until I thought of something to say. "She said your TV was acting up. Maybe you weren't getting all the channels and could I help, she said."

Her niece's name was Constance, but she went by Connie. And Connie said how much she liked my aunt's cooking and how sweet she was to have them both over.

I asked if they were having electrical problems after the storm.

Miss Imogene raised an eyebrow. "Why would you ask that?"

"Just noticed all the lights are off in the back is all," I said.

"Oh," she said.

"That's environmental," Connie said. "On account of the environment. We all have to pitch in and do our part."

I nodded. "Yeah. We all have to do our part."

We talked for a while longer about the weather. How hot it was going to get and how the weatherman said another big storm was coming that weekend.

"How's your aunt doing?" Miss Imogene asked.

"Fine, I guess. What do you mean?"

"I just mean, you know, what with your uncle's passing on like that."

"Oh. Yeah. Fine, I guess. I don't know. I mean, it's been a couple of years, you know?"

"I know," she said. "But that don't always matter, now does it?"

"No, ma'am. Guess it doesn't."

"Well, she'd best stay safe. Got a feeling in my bones all heck is about to break loose."

"Sure that ain't just rain coming?" I asked.

"You joke all you want, but you heard what happened up there on the hill. Those Sawyers and Pribbles cooking up all those drugs until the whole house exploded."

"Yes, ma'am. I heard about that. Awful."

"They had a show on the Fox channel a bit ago. Showed all these faces of these people on the drug. You know they cook that from cold medicine."

"Yes, ma'am. Just awful."

"Speaking of cooking." Connie said she'd found a recipe in an old *Southern Living* she'd gotten from the discard stack at the library in Magnolia. "I'm not much of a cook. But it's for this thing called a Kentucky Hot Brown."

"Connie," Miss Imogene said. "Ain't nobody got an inclination to cook for you. You can't just go inviting yourself over and expecting people to spend all their time and money serving you."

"People gotta eat. What's it matter if it's something good?"

Before Miss Imogene could fire back with anything, I stood up to go, thanked them for the drink, and put the recipe in my pocket.

Then I walked back to my Aunt Vee's to tell her I didn't know how to fix the antenna.

HOW MANY HOLES

The light was fading away as they pulled into town for gas. "Need anything?" he asked Loriella, climbing out of the truck.

She shook her head.

Randy Pribble reached into his pocket, counted out some singles. A Camaro squealed in on the other side of the pumps, engine rattling.

He put eleven dollars in the tank, walked in to pay. Saw a newspaper on the rack by the beef jerky. Picture of cops standing around a car, looking in the windows, red splatters from the inside. The story said the man had been laid off from some factory that morning. Father of three young boys. He drove around all day instead of going home. When five o'clock came, he pulled a pistol from the glove box, put a hole through his head. Above the car, the light had changed to green.

When Randy got back, the guy from the Camaro was leaning against a post, trying to talk to Loriella through the truck window. He was a big guy, skin tight like a child's balloon twisted into the shape of a man.

Randy coughed, walked up behind him. "You got a problem?"

The guy's shoulders jumped, and he took a step back. "No. No. Just . . . " he said, looking around the parking lot, "just saying 'hi.'"

"Well, maybe you oughta just shut your mouth, fatass."

"Yeah. Sure. No worries."

Behind Randy, a minivan had pulled up, slowed, rattled around a pothole, kept going. He watched the fat man walk into the store; then he took a breath, counted the potholes in the parking lot. One at the van. Thought about what Loriella was going through. That part of life where the pastor takes you by the shoulders and talks about how God never gives you more than you can handle. Two more potholes near the road. Same as we all go through. A couple along the back. And all you get are the little things to keep you going. A lottery ticket. A good dinner. And Randy with barely enough cash for dessert. Forget about dinner.

He saw the fat guy walking out of the store holding a piece of wood with the bathroom key. Thought about his car. That gold necklace with the cross. He watched the man turn the corner at the building, step out of the streetlight. Thought about the guy driving his Camaro through town, able to stop anywhere he wants to buy something. The sort of asshole who never checks his pockets before getting to the counter, never counts his change, never checks the soda machine for a loose quarter. The sort of asshole who goes to work on a Friday and puts twenty on the Cowboys because he thinks it's fun to gamble. The sort of asshole who gets into his Camaro after work and stops for dinner and those drinks they make with four or five ingredients.

Randy followed the man into the darkness.

Loriella was fingering the graduation cap tassel hanging from the rearview mirror when he got back into the truck.

He asked her was she all right.

"Not the same, is it? If I get my GED instead of walking."

"Diploma? You mean maybe you want to finish?"

"I don't know." She pushed the tassel away, rested her chin on her hand. "I just don't want to go back there, you know."

"Yeah. Nobody blames you."

"Blames me?" She turned to Randy as he pulled onto the highway. "Blame me for what?"

"For quitting," he said, checking traffic. "I mean for not going back. Hell, Keith ain't going back, neither."

"Yeah, I heard that. What about his scholarship? Wasn't he going to SAU?"

"I don't know. I don't think he's worried about that. He's still kinda messed up and shit."

"Yeah. A lot of us are."

"He was with her. You know, when all of y'all left the party. They were gonna, you know. Right? You know what I'm saying?"

"Of course I know." Loriella wiped her nose. "Staci was one of my best friends."

"Yeah."

"She was gonna be a phlebotomist, you know?"

"What's that?"

"Nurse who takes your blood."

"That right?" He nodded. "Like a vampire?"

She grinned, but just a little. "Something like that. Gonna make good money, too. Couple of years in college. She could have . . . " Loriella swallowed slowly, let the words trail off. "I never should have left her that night." She rubbed her eyes with the back of her wrist, mumbled out the window. Closed her eyes. "I was with her. I was with her. Right there."

"They'll find out what happened. It'll be okay." Randy watched the lights along the road as they drove in silence. The houses here and there. Satellite dishes in the yards. New cars in the driveways. Other people who went to college, learned skills you could put on a resume. He slid some cash across the seat to her. "Maybe we can have a little something to eat? We got a long night."

She picked up the wad of cash. "Well, aren't you Mr. Money-bags," she said.

He tapped the steering wheel. "Forgot about that, I guess."

She handed the money back to him. "Forget you're a Cowboys fan?"

"What?"

"The money clip. Must be a serious fan to have a Dallas Cowboys money clip."

"It was a gift," he said, scanning the signs for a decent restaurant.

"That right?"

"Yeah. Hey, you know where there's a good place to eat? All I know of is cheap hamburger places."

"There's that fancy Chinese place over other side of the court-house," she said.

"It nice?"

"Don't know. Never been."

"How about seafood?"

"Sure. Whatever's cool."

+ + +

She was putting another catfish bone into her napkin when the waitress came back.

"Would you care for any dessert?" she asked them.

"What you got?" Loriella asked, chomping each word as though she were chewing gum.

"Chocolate pie, lemon meringue. I think that's it."

Loriella smiled, raised her eyebrows at Randy.

"Go ahead, if you want," he said. "I'm done."

"Oh. That's okay," Loriella said. "No, thanks." Then she looked at the paintings on the wall. Mostly landscapes. A couple head shots.

When the waitress started to move away, he told her to bring a piece of everything.

Loriella reached her hand across the table to his. "Thank you for coming," she mouthed to him.

The waitress looked down to write on her notepad. "Oh, lord," she said. "What happened to your leg?"

He looked down at the outside of his pants leg, a splotch of blood the size of a hand. "Hunh," he said. "Dog got caught in some barbed wire this morning. Tore up a little."

"Oh, no. Is he okay?"

"Yeah," he said. "Better than my pants."

She smiled. "Oh, good. I'll get your pie."

They were finishing the pie when the waitress came back with the check.

"That man over there, the picture," Randy said. "That's the guy from *Apocalypse Now*, right? The boat captain took Martin Sheen up the river?"

"I don't know," she said. "Probably. He's in that TV show now with that guy who hopped in other people's bodies and that comedian with the bitchy wife."

He said all right.

"I think he used to live around here, maybe. It's Shelia's Uncle Albert. Want me to ask was he the fella in that movie? What did you say the name was?"

"Never mind. Don't matter."

✦ ✦ ✦

He put his arm across the back of the seat, turned to pull out of the parking lot. Watched her light a cigarette, run a comb through her hair.

"I still turn you on?" she asked.

He rubbed her shoulder, glad she wasn't thinking about any of the trouble. Told her she turned him on. Told her everything would be all right. Told her he was sorry. About all of it.

"You know the human body has three trillion pores?"

He sent the back of the truck over a curb, pulled into traffic. "What?"

"Pores. The little holes where sweat comes out. I saw it on the news. There's like three trillion on the human body."

"That seems like a lot."

"That's what I said. I was telling Darlene at the Dairy Queen and I said that was a lot and she said she wondered who counted them and I said that's silly. Don't nobody count all those pores. They just look at part of you and multiply."

"Yeah. I bet that's what they do."

"Still, awful lot of holes. It's a wonder we're able to hold anything inside us."

✦ ✦ ✦

They walked across the dirt to her mom's house, sky mostly black, poked open here and there with stars.

"I can do this, you want to wait in the truck," he said. "Won't take long."

"No. I know where it is. Wait here." She walked to the back of the house, came out with a little box.

"That's it?"

"Yeah. It'll be okay now," she said, climbing into the truck, easing the door closed.

"It will," he said. "It will be fine."

"You sure?"

He said he was. He told her how sometimes you just have to wait these things out. How maybe faith was all you had left sometimes, but you just had to wait. He told her the story of when he fell down into that well when he was a kid. How he knew he was okay when he pressed up against the wall, how he knew then the emptiness didn't go on forever. All holes have sides.

He wanted to tell her about how he had plans for both of them, after her mother got better. How he knew what everyone thought of his family. His brother. His uncle. His two dead cousins. He knew he should say something to her, something about Staci. Something about how the best thing they could do would be to get away from that life, those people. His family. Even the family he'd lost. You leave behind the living and the dead. You just do. You can't tie yourself to your family. You can't keep looking behind you. You have to leave behind everything that holds you back. And he was working on that, working on getting himself free of all that. You have to just look ahead, he thought. He wanted to tell her everything at once.

Instead he told her about the man in the car. How he gave up just before the light turned to green.

"That movie you were talking about," she said. "*Apocalypse Now*. We saw it in Mrs. Mitchell's class. That boat captain. He wants to turn around and get this girl to shore and the guy won't let him. The Martin Sheen guy shoots the girl and says keep moving."

"Yeah."

"So?"

"So what?" He'd turned onto the highway, heading to the hospital.

"So how do you know whether to shoot the girl and keep moving or just sit in the car and wait for the light to change?"

"I don't know." He took a breath. "You just know, I guess."

"When my dad died," she said and stopped. Opened the box. Looked inside.

"You never said what was in the box."

"Okay."

"Okay what?"

"Okay, I'll tell you. See, my dad never died. That's just what my mom said. He left. This is the box that my momma kept *her* momma's wedding ring in. My grandma's. In this box."

"So your mom wants the ring."

"I'd imagine." Then she held the box in front of Randy, shook it so he could hear it was empty. "No ring."

"I don't get it."

"When my daddy left, he took all our shit. Sold it, my momma said. Even my grandma's wedding ring."

"Jesus." Randy wanted to pull over, get a hold of her and pull her close. Say, "I know. I know." Just hold her tight against him until they were small enough to fit into a small box of their own, tucked away where no one could get to them. But he just kept driving.

"All she had was this box. Not even an antique or nothing. Just a box. She'd pull it down and look at it. Keep it around. For a while I thought it was just to remind herself of her mother, you know? Like a keepsake. Like where the ring used to be or whatever."

"Yeah."

"I asked her one time. She said it was where she'd put all her hopes. All her memories. In this box."

"Damn."

"I asked her another time. She said she just wanted to remember what she'd lost. Then she said she just wanted to keep an eye on all the shit she'd gone through. It's just an empty box, you know? You can put anything you want in it, I guess."

She opened the truck door and stepped down into the hospital parking lot.

The lights at the hospital flickered, settled into a hum. She held the box in her hands as she walked down the hall ahead of him, a little quicker with each step. A little further away.

DEBTS TO PAY

He took the last Oreo out of the jar, walked back to his chair in front of the television. After just twenty minutes, he was feeling like an expert on the secret Soviet aircraft of World War II.

Behind him, down the hall, he could hear his wife and a couple of women laughing, coughing for the past hour. He tried to calculate how many more perms she'd need to give before they could pay off the hair-dryer chair and the shampoo-basin chair he'd had to drive up to Little Rock to get. His unemployment check barely covered the gas money. Still, women liked to look nice. And his wife had been the most popular stylist at Shear Ecstasy in Magnolia before they decided to cut back her hours. Leaving and taking her clients with her.

Maybe they'd get the chairs paid off and he could redo the living room. Get rid of the paneling. Paint it. Peel it off. Put up some of the wainscoting they were talking about last night on that remodeling show. A chair rail.

He knew they'd never have the money for that. He'd had to spend most of what they had in the bank for an alternator he'd picked up at the salvage yard. Now the battery was acting up again. And his truck was coughing like one of the pistons was going. He'd pulled the plugs. Checked the valves and figured it was a problem with the pressure on one of them. He'd look again in a little bit to see if there was something he could do, but it was like last fall when they'd had the leak over the kitchen. Sometimes all you can do is look for a pot big enough to catch the water.

Maybe the beauty shop would take off. Maybe ladies would drive from an hour away to have their hair done. He'd heard a woman at prayer meeting say her sister the other side of Waldo had opened a shop and people all the way from Texarkana had regular appointments. Said she was going to put in a tanning bed come the fall. He'd listened to her story, nodded at the right spots, but he knew some people were just born lucky. And some weren't.

Something happens, the engine on the mower blows or you spend three straight days crapping blood, and you count back to the last bad thing. The tree through the porch. The rotten tooth. The burned-out relay in the septic tank. You ask yourself how other people do it. When it got so tough. How anyone ever gets ahead. Just a little, you say. Just a hundred bucks in a coffee can you won't have to go into in a month when something else goes wrong.

He reached across the table for the hospital bill. Call the 800 number in who the hell knows where to set up a payment plan within ten days or they'd turn it over to collections. He knew the drill. Tell them you'll pay twenty bucks a month for the next hundred years and they'd leave you alone. Which was all he really wanted.

He turned the envelope over and looked at the phone number he'd written down. He knew he shouldn't have done that. Just act like you're writing it down. Say, "Uh-huh. Got it. Thanks." Then hang up. Don't keep something like that around. That kind of temptation is just asking for trouble.

On the television, an image of Alexander Novikov faded in and out of airplane factories as the Soviets started building their forces. He'd watched the video a few times already. Knew the story of the air force commander who was stripped of his power and sent to a labor camp, then found his way back into favor.

Grady looked for connections in everything. Delsie wanted a mirror for the beauty shop, so he looked around Magnolia, Emerson, El Dorado for just the right one. In a thrift store he found one sitting on a VCR and remembered what Delsie had said a few days before. How she would have to miss her stories if women wanted appointments in the early afternoon. She'd miss *As the World Turns* and *Guiding Light*. He'd said they could get another television and put it in the shop, but she said she had to concentrate on her work.

"Besides," she said, "we don't have the money for another TV."

"We can find the money somehow," he said, but they both knew they couldn't.

He got the VCR for her as a surprise. A late anniversary present, he told her. When he set it up to record her stories last week, he found the Soviet aircraft tape wedged inside. The long black ribbon had pulled from the casing when he tried to free it. He had to cut it loose, then piece it back together, losing a few minutes about the Siege of Stalingrad about a half hour in.

He mouthed the numbers written on the envelope, stared at Novikov on the screen, looking for a connection. What was it like when everyone turned on you? What was it like in the labor camps? What was it like when you came back?

He set the envelope back down on the table, saw cookie crumbs on his shirt. He pushed himself out of the chair, walked back to the kitchen, opened the fridge, took a quick swig of milk, and put the container back. Looked for a toothpick to work something loose.

He heard one of the women in the back of the house cackle, "As if," and thought about how much they'd have to raise to buy a trailer from Herschel's place out on the highway. Couple thousand, probably. Then what? Lay a foundation. Run some current. She'd want sinks, of course. No, best just to keep the beauty shop in one room of the house for now. The women could laugh and jabber all they wanted. Could sneak across the hall and use the bathroom. He remembered he was supposed to empty the trash in the bathroom before she saw her first client.

He pulled a couple of plastic grocery store bags from under the sink, then walked down the hallway. The women were laughing about something, so he stopped by the beauty shop door to listen.

"Delsie," someone said to his wife, "you really have just done a lovely job here."

He heard his wife say, "Thanks."

The woman went on, talking about how successful the shop would be and how wonderful it was not to have to drive all the way into town now.

He heard his wife say his name, say that he'd gone up to Little Rock to get the chairs and how he'd spent the weekend painting and repainting the room. Three coats of Sunburnt Sky, with Lakehouse Lilac for the trim. "Wouldn't have thought," she said, "but he was right. The colors make the room pop."

Grady caught himself smiling like an idiot. They'd had their trouble, especially after he got laid off. But he felt things coming back together for him and Delsie. He'd read in a magazine that when your wife says, "I feel like we're not connected" the last thing you want to do is tell her she's wrong. When they first got married twenty years before, he'd have pointed to things they'd done that week. "Didn't we go out to dinner?" or "Didn't I tell you this morning how sweet you are?" Things like that to prove her wrong. When he'd gotten the VCR and mirror in El Dorado, the woman there had thrown in some magazines for free, so Grady took them home, read them like they were passed down from the Almighty. Maybe there was something in there he was supposed to read. Why else would she give them to him? Meant to be. There'd been some magazines for men, mostly old sports issues. One of the magazines, one about relationships and diets, had an article about seven ways to keep the romance alive. He didn't read the whole thing, but he skipped to the box with each idea numbered. The third one said that when your loved one says he or she doesn't feel connected—and he couldn't imagine a man saying that, but figured the magazine had to be politically correct these days—you don't want to prove him or her wrong. Just say "I feel that, too" and then suggest doing something together.

So when Delsie said that, he said he felt it too, and that they should have a picnic on the hill by the old barn.

Soon they were working on plans for her shop and he was helping her pick out paint and putting it all together. And it felt good to be working again.

Grady leaned on the washing machine in the hallway, listening to the women talk.

"Well," another one said, "that's good to hear. I was beginning to think he was good for nothing."

Then the women with his wife laughed. The women in the beautiful room.

The first woman, Grady recognized her as Birdie Cassels, said that maybe he could get a job as a painter.

"Like Picasso?" one of them joked.

"No," Birdie Cassels said. "Like one of those homosexuals on the TV."

Then the women laughed.

He set the bags down and listened for his wife, but she didn't say anything.

+ + +

He took a couple bags of trash around to the back of the house where the women had parked their cars, then tossed the bags into the bed of his truck, bungeed down the tarp.

Birdie Cassels's car was blocking him in. The shop was on the other side of the house, so he couldn't even knock at the window without walking around the house, feeling like an ass.

She'd brought the car to the church homecoming a few weekends before. A Platinum Cadillac DTS, the replacement for the DeVille line, she'd explained to everyone. "The largest luxury car they make," she said. People lined up like it was a tour of Hot Springs, and she drove a few people at a time around the loop and back. Finally, Delsie and Berta Mae were the only two who hadn't gone and had to give in.

"Very nice," Delsie had said. "You're lucky to have a nice car like that."

Birdie Cassels laughed. "Oh, sugar. Lucky? My poor Jed works fifty hours a week at the office so we don't starve to death. And I just had to get a new car. You know how unreliable cars can get when they turn two or three years old."

Delsie just nodded and walked down to the dessert end of the tables to find Grady and tell him about the car.

Grady stood behind his house while the women were getting their hair done and wondered what sort of protective coating the Cadillacs came with. Then he unzipped his jeans and peed along the passenger's door, cleaning the grime off the shining silver.

Grady had been standing at the corner of the house for a few minutes, wondering whether to go back inside to get the envelope with the phone number on it. Wondering if it was the right thing to do. He'd written it down, so maybe it was meant to be, he thought, knowing it wasn't. Knowing it was probably one of those moments you look back on years later, thinking if just this one thing hadn't happened, how different it would all be. Like the months after the problem at the Dixie Mart that time. If he'd just backed out. Said it was a bad idea. Or if he'd seen the woman and her kid in time. Or if they'd been five minutes later.

He hadn't thought about that night in years. Hadn't had reason to. He'd had a good job and a clean record since then. A good home. A wife who loved him.

Grady heard the rattle-pop of tires on gravel, looked up to see Cleovis Porterfield coming down the road, clouding out exhaust and dust, turning his '69 Camaro into the drive and stopping. Grady waved at him, so Cleo got out of the car, walked toward the house.

Cleo nodded to the back of the house and the makeshift parking lot. "Delsie kick you out of the Tupperware party?"

Grady felt something in the back of his mouth, then gave up trying to get at it with the tip of his tongue. "Beauty shop."

"Thought she quit."

"Relocated."

"Ah," Cleo said, nodding. "Speaking of relocating—"

Grady swallowed. "Yeah. I got the message. Just haven't called him back."

"You gonna?"

"Dunno," Grady said, leaning back against the house, feeling the bricks pinch through his thin T-shirt. His lucky shirt from the Muleriders' win at the Aztec Bowl back in 1990. He'd gone to some night classes that year at SAU and followed the team. Went to some games as though he belonged. This last year hadn't been too good for the team. Even the Baptist college had beaten them. Hell, hadn't been too good for a lot of people.

"Good money in it for us," Cleo said. "For you."

"Yeah. I know about the money. Just trying to stay on the right path these days, you know."

Cleo walked around to the other edge of the driveway, looked out past the fence where acres and acres had been clear-cut by the loggers. "Everybody needs money, Grady. Unless you're just going to get your money from Delsie."

"That supposed to mean?"

"Nothing. Just saying she brings in the money, what's left for you to do?"

"You know I been looking. Had an interview last Tuesday but the woman called to say they already filled it before I even got a chance to talk to the man."

"Yeah. That's the way it goes."

Grady nodded. That is the way it goes.

"It's just a job," Cleo said. "Just one little favor for Sawyer. And it ain't like you don't owe him."

Grady straightened up. "Everybody owes everybody these days."

Cleo nodded. Everybody owes everybody.

"Besides," Grady said, "it's not just a job, Cleo. You know that. If it was just a job he'd get some other guys to do it."

"You know he can't get anyone else. Can't go with the regular guys. This has to be handled, whatever the phrase is. Whatever it was he said."

"Out of the network?"

"Yeah," Cleo said. "That's what he said."

"Not so sure I can help him out on this one," Grady said. Then he looked over at the parked cars by his house. He knew he'd have to wait until the women left to make his trip to the dump. Maybe things would work out. Maybe he could find something there. A couple of months before he'd found a boy's bicycle on the edge of the metal junk pile at the dump. The new guy had made a fuss about recycling, but eventually let Grady bring it home. He'd cleaned it up, meaning to sell it at the Emerson flea market some weekend. Maybe someday he would. Maybe he'd hear of someone wanting to buy a boy's bicycle. Maybe some woman would say something to Delsie and then she'd tell them her husband has a bicycle for sale. Maybe things would work out that way, he thought.

You just bide your time. Like Alexander Novikov. Have faith. One day they'll bring a car to the labor camp and take you home. One day a lady will hand you a magazine with an article you need to read. Everything happens for a reason. One day your wife will tell you someone wants whatever you've been working on. One day it all falls into place when your wife comes to tell you that, a sign that everything is going to work out just fine.

Cleo took a pack of cigarettes out his pocket, offered one to Grady. "Here."

Grady swallowed, shook his head. "Promised Delsie I'd give them up. Bad for you. Bad for the wallet."

"All right," Cleo said, sliding a cigarette from the pack for himself.

Grady heard a window slide open on the other side of the house as Delsie let some of the hair fumes out, thought about how they'd talked about improving the ventilation in the room. He knew she'd bring something up tonight. Say the women had been complaining about it, coughing, sputtering like an old truck.

One day you're driving to Little Rock to get chairs for your wife and she says you're the best husband in the world and you take her in your arms and she kisses your ear and your neck and your mouth and she pushes you back into the chair and unbuttons her shirt and you know, you just know, this is the best day of your life.

And then one day she doesn't say anything.

Grady stuck the tip of his tongue back in his teeth, found the little piece that had been bothering him. He worked it loose, spit it down at his feet.

"Wait," he said to Cleo. "I could use a smoke."

COUNTRY
HARDBALL

Hank Dalton walked around the outside wall of the Rebel Mini-Mart while the deputy asked him questions.

"So you can't think of any former employees you let go recently? Maybe someone knew the schedules?"

Dalton had been squatting at the corner of the building, stood up, holding a cigarette butt in his hand. "No."

The deputy made some notes, then waited for Dalton to explain the cigarette. He gave up. "That cigarette mean something, Mr. Dalton?"

"No idea, son." Dalton put the butt in the front pocket of his blazer.

"That might be evidence," the deputy said.

"How long you boys been here?" Dalton asked him, walking back to the front doors of the mini-mart.

"About an hour."

"Who's left? You and Skinny Dennis?"

"Yes, sir. Myself and Deputy McWilliams."

"You fellas about to pick up the cigarette butts? You best get started."

The deputy looked around, saw dozens of butts against the edge of the building in all directions. "Maybe we could just go inside and I could ask a couple more questions."

"Where's Katie Mae?"

"She's in back of the store. Deputy McWilliams is interviewing her now."

Dalton stopped halfway through the doorway. "Skinny Dennis is talking to Katie Mae? Alone?"

"Yes, sir."

"You sure that's all right?" Dalton asked.

"Oh, no problem. He's a deputy now. And, you know, all that was years ago."

"Yeah, but the McMahen girl. You know? How's he taking that?"

"'Bout like you'd expect, I guess," the deputy said.

Behind the store, Deputy Dennis McWilliams and Katie Mae sat next to each other on a railroad tie against the back wall. They looked out across the dirt path curling behind the store, the weedy field, the train tracks that led somewhere else.

"How you feeling?" he asked her. He figured she was maybe seventeen. Working after school and weekends. Saving up to go to college in Magnolia in the fall. Maybe she had a scholarship. Maybe she was one of those kids things fell in place for.

"Still a little, I don't know, worked up? Like shaky feeling, I guess."

"Okay." McWilliams took out a cigarette, offered it to the girl. He'd had to give them up recently, but he carried a pack with him for times like these.

"Starting to get a little mad, you know? Like what the hell?" She took the cigarette. He lit it for her, holding her hands steady.

"Sounds about right."

"What do you mean?"

"The stages of grief. The fear and then the anger. First is shock, I guess. Then fear and anger. Then the last is acceptance."

"Oh. Guess I'm right on schedule?"

"Yeah, sounds like it."

"Happens to a lot of people."

"Getting robbed? Yeah. More than you'd think."

"Wait." She squinted an eye, tilted her head. "I thought there were more stages."

"That's alcoholics," he said. "They get twelve."

"Oh. Guess I'm lucky I'm not an alcoholic."

"Lucky."

"You ever know any alcoholics?"

"Yeah. I probably have."

"My dad's girlfriend was an alcoholic," she said. "The one he was seeing last year. Had a nose ring."

"She had a what?"

"Nose ring."

"Like a big hoop hanging out?"

She shook her head. "No. Like a little stud."

"What's so weird about that?" he asked her. "I used to know this chick with a tongue ring."

"I just kept looking up at her nose thinking she had some booger in there. Wondering if I should say something the whole time she was talking." Then she laughed. McWilliams counted that as a good sign. Katie Mae grinned at him.

"A booger on the outside of her nose?" he asked.

"No. On the inside, looked like. Musta been the back of the nose ring."

"Oh, right."

They sat that way for few minutes, looking out at the train tracks as if something was going to come along.

"So," she said, "this chick with the tongue ring. Like for doing stuff on a guy down there?"

"How do you know about things like that?" He almost called her "Katie Mae," but knew that would sound like he was scolding her. And he'd done such a good job getting her trust, he thought.

"I know stuff," she said. "I'm not a kid."

"Okay." He wanted to tell her she was and that there wasn't anything wrong with that. Damn, what he wouldn't give to be her age again. Like a piece of cheese that's gone bad, you just cut off the side that's got the mold. The last however many years. And you're left with a good piece of cheese again.

"So she got the tongue thing for pleasing her man?"

"No," McWilliams said, wondering how grown-up Katie Mae was. "This chick was a lesbo."

"No shit?"

"No shit."

Katie Mae nodded, taking the cigarette out of her mouth. "Cool."

Deputy Owen Caskey came around the corner, clearing his throat, as McWilliams was handing Katie Mae another cigarette. "Time to move along," Caskey said.

Katie Mae and McWilliams stood up together, dusted off their pants. She said thanks for the talk, and he handed her his card from his shirt pocket. "If you think of anything," he said.

On the drive back to the sheriff's department, McWilliams stared out the window at his own reflection while Caskey scrolled through what he knew.

"You paying attention to what I'm saying?" he asked McWilliams.

"Yeah. That all you got?"

"And the cigarette Dalton picked up. That and the description of the perps."

"Perps?"

"Perpetrators."

Jesus, McWilliams thought. "Nobody says 'perps' except on the television."

"Shut up."

"Sorry. On the 'boob tube.'"

"Just shut up. Like you know everything."

"So you watch the surveillance tape?" McWilliams asked.

"Yeah. Pretty good quality, you know?"

"You see faces?"

"Naw, they were both wearing those deer-hunting masks."

"Those what?"

"Orange toboggans."

"You sure?"

"Yeah. Got that from the kid before you took her out back. Said they were orange."

"Okay."

"You get anything out back?"

"What's that supposed to mean?"

"Anything about the perps?"

McWilliams let it go. "She didn't recognize them. Their movements. Their accents. Said it was like they were trying to sound British or Australian. She'll remember something once the shock wears off."

"Hope so."

"How much they get?"

"Dalton said about $150 out of the register. Wasn't sure what they'd taken from the office. Said he'd do an inventory once MeChell gets there. She does his insurance." Caskey stopped the car at a light, grabbed a fast-food napkin from the console, and put it in the bottom of his empty Styrofoam cup. Pulled a can of dip from his shirt pocket, slid it between his fingers, and thumped it back and forth for a few seconds. Twisted the lid off, wedged a clump under the left side of his bottom lip. Wiped his lips with his thumb, blew loose flakes into the air. Started to swallow a few times, then spit a grainy brown string of juice into the cup. "You ever see her? That MeChell? Shit, that's a nice piece of ass."

Dennis got home, opened the front door to a room of middle-aged women who stopped talking all at once.

Cora stood up, walked to her husband. "Catch any bad guys?" She kissed him on the cheek.

"Every last one," Dennis said, then nodded to the room. "Ladies."

The half dozen of them said hello, and he and Cora walked into the kitchen.

"I invited them over after the prayer meeting," she said, then moved to a whisper. "Janeva's daughter's done run off." Then a deeper whisper, leaning in, "With a black boy."

Dennis sat down at the table with a can of soda from the ice-box. "Which daughter?"

"The youngest."

Dennis nodded. He knew the kid. He'd had to talk to the girl a few times in the parking lot of Walker's Grocery on Saturday nights. Kids cruising from one end, down through what was left of the town to the football field, then back to Walker's parking lot. Warm beer and fistfights. Shirtless teenage boys circling each other, backward caps for baseball teams they never watched, leaning back as they moved, tensing up and swinging blind until someone got caught in the nose or ear and they both went down in a heap of headlights and gravel. The girls in cutoffs and tank tops, sitting up in truck beds, leaning against car hoods, until the deputies or town cops came rolling up to catch whoever got blocked in.

Dennis had seen Janeva's youngest, Treena, just last weekend, had talked to her about keeping away from trouble, watching out for the wrong crowd. He knew it had sounded dumb at the time. And he'd say, "I know this sounds dumb," but he'd go on. He wanted to tell her how he knew, how he should have told his kid sister the same thing. It mattered. The saying of the thing. The explaining. It mattered that he never got to tell his sister, that he could have. Should have. Told her how you'd come to find out what it was like being with the wrong crowd when it was too late and you're falling down a hill, and there's not a damn thing you can do but wonder where the wrong step you'd made was. How one night it can all turn. You'll be with the boy, he wanted to tell her, and you'll want one thing and he'll want another and before either of you knows what's going on, it's all over for you and for the boy and there's nothing left but for the families to hate each other. That one night. Just like this night.

And one day your brother or somebody will be grown up, married to a wonderful woman, and have a job, a good job. A job with crappy hours and crappy pay, but a job where he can make a difference. Maybe not enough of a difference. Not the sort of difference that changes anything that has already happened. Maybe something.

Or maybe not a damn bit. He can spend his nights talking to kids in parking lots, giving twenty-minute presentations to school assemblies, and still you'll walk right out into the darkness. And all he can do is write things down in a notebook, talk to people until he gets to "the last one to see her alive." And he can try to pull her back from that person, that last person, look for something there, some thread that he can grab hold of and pull, as if it were something tangible. As if all the effort mattered at all when something had already been done. As if knowing who was to blame made anything better. As if getting the answer to a question, any question, was any sort of comfort. Sitting in the "family room" at the station, next to the McMahens, listening to Nate say how the state won't rest until the guilty are punished. As if there would ever be enough punishment.

Cora had been talking. "So we have to keep Janeva's mind off it, you know?"

"Sure."

"Not that we're racist," she said, for what Dennis took as no reason at all. "But you know how people can talk. Young white girl with a black boy."

"Yeah."

"Like that Chip Steele on Channel Seven," Cora said. "We were just talking about him. Nobody has any problem with him. And he's black."

"Yeah," Dennis nodded. "He is."

"And he seems like a nice black man. Very well spoken."

"The sports guy?"

"Yes, sweetie. Weren't you listening?"

"Sorry, it's been a long day."

"Selia said she heard on the scanner. Robbery at the mini-mart. That girl working?"

"Yeah."

"You talk to her?"

"It's fine. She's fine."

"She get hurt?"

"No, just shaken up."

Cora started to say something. She opened her mouth, made that little pop when her lips parted, but swallowed whatever it was.

He knew what was coming. "Don't get all upset about it," he said. "It's fine."

"Dennis, I'm not upset," Cora said. "I just . . . " She sat down at the table, put her hand on his. "I just know how you want to help. How you can get involved with these kids. Like the McMahen girl."

"Can we not talk about it, please?"

She pulled her hand back and stood up. "Why won't you let me help?"

"I'm fine," he said. "Nothing to help with."

Cora walked back to the living room, started talking to her friends. Dennis touched a drop of condensation on the side of the can, watched it run into another drop, then fall to the bottom. "I'm fine," he said again.

✦ ✦ ✦

The next morning, Dennis and Caskey drove back to the mini-mart to talk to Hank Dalton.

"You know who gets out today?" McWilliams asked.

"Sorry. Forgot to read the reports this morning while I was laying cable."

"Laying cable?"

"Sorry. Taking a shit. Dropping the kids off at the pool. It's a euphemism. Damn, man. Yesterday I can't say 'perps' and today I can't say a fucking euphemism?"

"Mosley."

"Which one?"

"Only one you put in jail this year."

"Hell, I didn't put him in jail," Caskey said. "Why do I always get blamed for shit? He's the one put his own self in trouble. I ain't judge and jury, you know? Hell, I'm a lot of damned things, but I ain't goddamn judge and jury."

"You arrested the man for breaking into his own house."

"Now, damn it. You're starting to sound just like the newspaper. You know damn well the bank owned that house."

"His house."

"Hell, no. The bank's house."

"You own your house?" McWilliams asked. "I got to send a $600 check every month to the bank. Guess it's their house. You going to arrest me, too?"

Caskey made the turn at 58 and slowed as he passed the Baptist church that had had three break-ins the past year. Quiet today. "No, you don't have to worry because you're making payments. Mosley wasn't."

"You know full well Littleton Mosley's wife screwed him over. He's working ten-hour shifts in Arkadelphia, and she's at home paying bills."

"Not my problem."

"No, and it wouldn't have been his problem if she'd been doing that instead of spending her day with the Pribble boy."

"That's the one she run off with? The kid mules for Rudd?" Caskey asked.

"Yeah."

"How you know so much about all this?"

"Because they went to our church. Mosley and his wife. His wife doesn't pay the bills and runs off with Pribble. Then you bust the man for going into his own house."

"Six months she didn't pay the mortgage, Dennis. You know that ain't right. Bank forecloses and padlocks the place. I didn't do that. Mosley breaks the locks open. I didn't do that."

"The bank locked up all his stuff in that house. His clothes. His mama's wedding ring. Everything the man owned. How was he supposed to know his wife wasn't paying the bills? That she was supporting Pribble?"

"You ask me, a man's gotta notice that kind of shit goes on in his own home. You know?"

"Yeah. Then it's a good thing I'm not asking you."

"Look, I just arrested him because someone called in a B&E. I was just doing my job. The bank's the ones what pressed charges. Blame them. Judge Gordon. He's the one what gave the guy thirty days. Blame him. Hell, I was just doing my job."

Yeah, McWilliams thought. That's what the judge and the bank would say, too.

"You see the game last night?" Caskey asked, trying to change the subject.

"Day game," McWilliams said. "Cora taped it."

"Conors starting, right?"

"Yeah. The Reds brought back their closer. Kid from Puerto Rico. Dominican. Whatever. Gets his head screwed on straight, he'll be a good one."

"Good fastball? Like really fast, right?" Caskey asked. He didn't much understand baseball.

"Fastball's fine. Good off-speed stuff, too. When he's on, not many better."

"What's he throw? Like a hundred?"

"Mid-90s, I think. It's not about speed. It's timing. It's control."

"A strike going 95 miles an hour is—"

"Is a goddamn walk-off homer in the major leagues," McWilliams said, then slapped the inside of the car door. He held his hand up, made a fist. Tightened it. Loosened it.

"You all right?" Caskey asked.

"Yeah."

"Good thing that's not your throwing hand," he said, then shut up quick.

When the deputies got to Dalton's store, the only customer was walking back to his truck, an old Chevy with a dog chained in the bed and a back window made from duct tape and a trash bag.

"Ossifurs," he nodded, then spit as they passed.

McWilliams reached back, grabbed the man's arm, leaned him against the hood of his truck while the dog started to break nasty.

"Might want to show a little respect there," McWilliams said.

The man kept his mouth shut, nodded. Swallowed a mouthful of dipspit before he was turned loose. The man peeled gravel as he left the parking lot.

Caskey held the door open as McWilliams walked through the front of the store, leaned in as he walked by. "You know that's one of Rudd's boys, right?"

McWilliams nodded, let his eyes adjust to the inside of the store. "That'll be just fine."

They each gave a two-finger eyebrow salute to the Tompkins kid behind the counter and walked toward the back where Dalton kept his office.

"How's Ruby doing?" McWilliams asked.

"She's doing all right, thanks. Good days and bad. Mostly good the past few weeks."

"Glad to hear that. Had her on the prayer list long enough, she oughta be damn near indestructible by now."

Dalton nodded. "Damn near is, I reckon."

"They still working on that class action suit against the mill? What'd she have in at that place? Thirty years?"

"She put in twenty-three-and-a-half years there. And the suit's about dead. Lawyers working out some sort of settlement with the government. Probably wind up asbestos is good for you, sprinkle it on your Wheaties, by the time they're done."

"No kidding?"

"Yeah. As long as the lawyers get their money, guess they don't mind. So you boys find out anything?"

Caskey looked for a place to spit, got most of it into a trash can. "Just had to ask you a couple of questions as follow-up, Hank."

"So you don't have anything?"

McWilliams took over while Caskey went back into the main store to grab a cup from the fountain drinks.

"My partner says you picked up some filters around the side of the store?"

"Yeah, place gets mighty trashified you're not careful."

"I was thinking maybe these were special. You still have them?"

"Why would I still have trashed smokes?"

McWilliams turned behind him as he heard Caskey getting close. He nodded, closed the door with Caskey on the outside. Figured Caskey could go make small talk with the Tompkins kid. McWilliams sat down in a folding chair and motioned for Dalton to do the same.

McWilliams leaned forward with his elbows on his knees, legs spread apart. "How long you known me for, Hank?"

"Shit, Dennis. What's this about?"

"My whole life, right?"

"Yeah. What are you getting at?"

"You know everybody, I bet. You worked the shop over at Emerson for years, working for your daddy. Then you took over. Got a couple more stores. All that time, you're in these stores, right? You know everybody."

"Yeah, I guess."

"You know Miss Velma? Sunday school teacher?"

"You know I do."

"She come in here ever?"

"Time and again, yeah."

McWilliams nodded. "What's she get?"

"Hell, I don't know."

McWilliams stood up, knocked his chair down behind him. "Damn it, Hank, we don't have all day. What the hell does Miss Velma buy?"

Hank Dalton leaned back, slid his chair a little. "Quart of milk. Saltines. *Soap Opera Digest.*"

"Goddamn right she does."

"What's that got to do with anything?"

McWilliams walked around Dalton's desk, opening drawers while Dalton said "hey now" and "you can't." Then from the middle drawer he pulled out a plastic bag of three cigarette butts, dumped them onto Dalton's desk.

McWilliams scooped them up in the palm of his right hand, held them in front of Dalton's face. "Who smokes these cigarettes?"

Caskey opened the door. "Everything all right, fellas?"

Neither man looked at Caskey. Both men nodded.

Caskey shut the door and walked back to talking with the Tompkins boy and McChell Womack, who'd come in to talk to Dalton about his insurance claim.

"I gotta bag some more ice," the kid said. "Holler anyone comes in." He walked to the back of the store.

"So," Caskey said, hopping up to sit on the counter, the only clear space next to the register, between the beef jerky and the energy boosts. "You were saying how you and Dwayne were done broke up."

"Deputy, I can't really see how that's any of your business, if you don't mind my saying."

"No, no. Not at all. Lotta folks don't understand how intertwined everything around here is."

"Intertwined?"

"Means linked together."

"I know what the word means," she said. "I just don't know how you mean it."

"Like look around. Man works his whole life making a good living. Goes the straight and narrow. Has all kinds of wicked shit he has to overcome, him and his wife. Pardon my French. The oldest boy. I mean, a parent shouldn't never have to bury their kid, right? And then he has some no-acccount younger boy gets everything handed to him his whole life, grows up the world owes him a living. Only he ain't never had to do a lick of work, you see?"

"Are you talking about Mr. Dalton's son?"

"I'm just talking out loud. You know, showing how one life intertwines with another. House of cards. Dominos. However you want to look at it. One thing tied up into the next, pull a thread and it all falls apart. How if I knew what so-and-so was doing at the time of the robbery, I could eliminate myself a suspect. All pieces to the same puzzle, only I ain't got the front of the box to see what the picture looks like."

"That's the only reason you were asking if Dwayne and I were still together? To see if I had an alibi for the robbery?"

"That's it exactly. See, I knew all that college learning would pay off for you."

"Two years in Magnolia isn't exactly 'all that college learning,' you know."

"Yeah. I went up there for some classes, too. Criminal justice. Wrote a paper on the hegemony of the justice system."

"The what?" she asked.

"Yeah. I never really got what it meant, neither. Something about power of some people over another. I remember the word, though. Hegemony."

"Oh. Well, the paper? That went okay?"

"I don't know. I just kinda stopped going. Like church, I guess. Two nights a week. The drive up there and back. You know, gas prices and all."

She nodded. "Don't I know it."

They sat there in silence for half a minute.

Caskey bounced the backs of his boots against the counter wall. Ba-dum-bump. Ba-dum-bump. "So I hear there's going to be a bunch of trouble this weekend."

She said, "Yeah?"

"Yeah. Figure you might want to have an alibi."

"To be safe?"

"Yeah. Just to be safe."

"You got any ideas?"

He grinned. "I got a few."

The office door opened. McWilliams and Dalton came into the main room of the store, the deputy holding one of the cigarette butts. Dalton went behind the counter, reached up into the cigarette display, and pulled out a package of Carolina Selects. He set them on the counter as Caskey slid off. McWilliams walked over, took the pack, wedged it into his shirt pocket.

"That's four and a quarter," Dalton said.

McWilliams turned to face him. "Put it on my tab, Hank. And tell Ruby we're praying for her." Then he moved for the door. "Miss Womack," he nodded and walked out, with Caskey trailing.

When they pulled out onto the street, Caskey asked him what that was all about.

"Hank knows who did it," McWilliams said.

"His boy?"

"No, don't think so."

"Why not? And what was all that about the cigarettes?"

"If he'd thought it was his boy again, he'd've given us someone else. Pointed us somewhere away from the boy. Like with the thing at his house. When he said it was a couple of drunk Mexicans."

"I don't follow."

"Well, when he told us that, I figured it was anybody *but* a couple of drunk Mexicans. Just sending us on a wild goose chase."

"Oh, I got ya," Caskey said, though he wasn't sure he did. "And the cigarettes?"

"Dalton picked up the butts by the store," McWilliams said. "You told me that. And you said he didn't throw them away."

"Yeah. Right. Put them in his pocket."

"How many trash cans have you seen between where he found those butts and his office?"

"Trash cans. I don't know. A couple?"

"Two outside. One inside the front door. And then the other one in his office. You need to pay more attention you looking for that promotion."

"Yeah. Okay. So what?"

"So, when you're cleaning up trash, what do you do?"

"Oh, I see. You throw it away. But he put the butts in his pocket."

"Right."

"Why'd he do that?"

"Right."

"Oh."

They made a couple of turns, pulled up to the sheriff's department. When McWilliams moved to get out, Caskey reached across for his arm. "So Hank was protecting someone?"

"That's what I figure."

"But it wasn't his son?"

"No. His son doesn't smoke Carolina Selects. Doesn't smoke at all."

"Maybe it was someone with him?"

"I don't think so. If it was Marlboros or Camels or a dozen other brands, who knows? But there ain't but so many people even remember Carolina Selects, much less smoke them."

"So you know who it was?" Caskey asked.

"Damn sure wasn't a couple of drunk Mexicans."

They got out of the car in time to see Deputy Mike Lacewell talking on his cell phone, walking toward his cruiser.

When he saw Caskey and McWilliams, Lacewell flipped his phone closed, slid it into his shirt pocket. "Fellas, just in time to turn your asses around. Got ourselves a search warrant."

Caskey whispered over the top of the cruiser to McWilliams. "Five bucks it's Dalton's kid."

"Where we headed?" McWilliams asked Lacewell.

"You'll never guess."

"Then how about you fucking tell us," Caskey said.

"Asshole. Heading to the Rudd farm."

"Damn," Caskey said, as soon as he could say anything.

They got back into the car and followed Lacewell.

McWilliams had pulled the shotguns from the trunk and was loading them as they drove. "This seem strange to you?" he asked Caskey.

"What do you mean?"

"Going in on a search warrant to Rudd's. You ever been to Rudd's farm on a warrant?"

"No."

"Ever tried?"

"Yeah."

"So why now?" McWilliams asked. "Why are we going in now?"

State troopers had already set up a barricade at the end of Rudd's road, the long, exposed drive up to the big house. Caskey slowed as they were waved through.

"Hell if I know," Caskey said. "I'm sure you got an idea."

"A couple," McWilliams said, sliding in another shell. "Maybe we get there and the place is totally clean. He sets this up, Rudd does, just to show he's got nothing to hide."

"That's smart."

"The kind of thing he'd do, right? Then next time someone tries to say he's the kingpin around here, he throws his hands up and says haven't we been through this, blah, blah, blah."

"Damn, that is smart." Caskey slowed down as the made a big curve up to Rudd's. "What else? You said you had a couple ideas?"

"Yeah. But I won't know until we get there. Lacewell got the warrant?"

"Don't know."

"All right. Can't know until then."

They got out of the car, walked across the side yard under a pecan tree. McWilliams reached down, picked up a pecan, bounced it in his throwing hand, let it fall to the ground.

They found Lacewell and some troopers by the front steps leading up to the porch. "Sheriff said tell you Eddie's with Mr. Rudd in the kitchen," he said.

"That mean you're supposed to keep me away from the kitchen?" McWilliams asked.

"Means you're supposed to keep your own damn self away from the kitchen. Oh, and before I forget, Mattie said Cora called at the office for you. Said don't forget dinner at Grady and Delsie's place."

"Yeah. Fine," McWilliams said. Salisbury steaks and cans of tea at his wife's brother's house. He planned to take his pistol in case someone said they were going to play Rook again. McWilliams looked up at the house, generations old, turned back to Lacewell. "Who's got a copy of the warrant?"

"Reckon there's plenty copies floating around so's we can tell what we're looking for."

McWilliams looked at the copy Lacewell was handing him. Date and address. Areas to be searched. The primary residence. All outbuildings, known and unknown, including but not limited to the "big barn." The place most of southwest Arkansas knew as the drying house. Stories of pot plants hung through like tobacco, hanging and drying. The place was cursed. Every time the cops got a good lead and followed it to the farm, they'd find nothing. Not even no drugs. Just an absence of everything. Cleaned up and all the good stuff hidden, like your in-laws were coming to visit. Even the aerial shots of the property had disappeared from the system.

"How'd we end up here?" McWilliams asked. "Why today?"

Lacewell laughed. "This ruin your plans? Got tickets for the big game?"

McWilliams was still reading through the warrant, but he saw Caskey swallow something thick. Look "what the hell?" at Lacewell.

"I meant the tractor pull," Lacewell said. "That tractor pull." Not the Astros exhibition game in Magnolia. Not the team Skinny Dennis could have been pitching for if he hadn't lost out on that scholarship, the draft, the Muleriders, the plan to hit the farm system after his degree. All to chase after whoever shot his little sister and that Rudd boy with her, asking for trouble. Not what Lacewell said at all.

"Where's Boggs?"

"Judge Boggs?" Lacewell asked.

McWilliams held the paper back out for Caskey. "He off hunting?"

"Maybe he's hunting for that piece of tail you let get away," Caskey said to Lacewell.

"Oh, shut up."

"Olivia?" McWilliams asked. "The woman in the clerk's office there?"

Caskey nodded. "She's fair game, right, Mike?"

"We're not going out now, if that's what you mean," Lacewell said.

"That's what I was asking."

McWilliams nodded. "So His Honor?"

"Think he's got cases tomorrow. I'm on the schedule to work the court." Lacewell was the type who liked working as a bailiff. Stand in one place. Air conditioning. A sit-down lunch with a knife and fork.

"Gordon signed the warrant," McWilliams said. "Should have been Boggs." Caskey was reading through the warrant, McWilliams grabbed it back. "Son of a bitch," he said. "We're looking for cash and a pistol. You see the list of what we're looking for?" McWilliams handed the warrant back to Caskey again.

"So what?" Caskey asked.

"Boggs handles the multijurisdictional grand jury," McWilliams said.

Caskey snorted. "'Handles' is right."

"What's that mean?" Lacewell asked.

"How many times you been out here?" McWilliams asked him.

"I don't know. Last year we were out here. Didn't find anything but a couple of stray dogs."

"Before that?"

"Every year for a while, I guess. Never find anything. Don't figure we'll find nothing this time."

"So why the hell are we out here again if every time we come, the place is clean?" Caskey asked.

"Different this time. Robbery. Not drugs," Lacewell said.

"And this time we'll find something," McWilliams said. "Hey, what's Rudd's connection to the robbery anyway?"

"Don't know," Lacewell said. "Some kid just found the orange toboggan at the end of the driveway. He'd heard the story on the radio so he called it in. Bing, bam, boom, here we are."

Big Gene walked up behind Lacewell, smacked him in the shoulders. "You ladies talking about your vaginas?"

"Hey, Gene," Caskey said, taking a step away. "Shouldn't you be up at the house, giving a statement like your boss, Mr. Rudd?"

"Done did," he said. "Figured I'd come down and see what you bunch of fairies were doing."

Caskey turned to McWilliams. "He seem drunk and disorderly to you?"

"Resisting arrest, too, right?" McWilliams said.

"Shit, fellas, what put you in a bad mood?" Then Gene leaned down into Lacewell's face, put his hand over his own mouth as if he were going to throw up. "Oh, hell, I see now. Looking at this guy in daylight is enough to make you sick."

Lacewell slapped Gene's hand away. "I'll have you know, big brother, I'm a duly deputized officer of the law."

Gene laughed. "May well be, but you're still so butt ugly even a priest wouldn't fuck you."

"All right," McWilliams said, taking Gene by the elbow. "You've had your fun." He walked with him out of earshot. "You come down here for any reason?"

"Boss says he doesn't want any trouble."

"That's good."

"Says if there's any trouble, he ain't starting it, you understand?"

"When is this trouble he isn't starting going to start?"

"My guess?"

McWilliams nodded.

"Right about the time those two troopers walk into the barn." Gene cocked his head, pointing behind him. McWilliams looked over Gene's shoulder to see two state troopers and someone in a blue FBI blazer about fifty yards in front of the barn, walking toward it.

Gene walked off and McWilliams turned back to Lacewell and Caskey. "Tell those troopers to stop right now."

"What?" Lacewell asked.

"Just tell them to hold up. Barn's hot."

"Shit," Lacewell said, running to the house and pulling out his radio.

Caskey stood next to McWilliams. "That Gene's good people."

"That Gene's an asshole."

"Yeah," Caskey said.

McWilliams saw the cops near the barn turn and walk back to the house. Then he heard the thumps of the helicopter coming overhead to land near the barn.

"You know," Caskey said, "I got my sniper certification on Tuesday. I could neutralize this situation from three times this distance."

"Good thing it didn't come to that."

"Yeah. But it woulda been sweet."

✦ ✦ ✦

On the way back to town, Caskey pulled in at the Rebel Mini-Mart.

"Was gonna get an ice cream sandwich," he said. "Want something?"

McWilliams shook his head. "Wouldn't imagine MeChell is still there."

"Worth a look."

When Caskey went inside, McWilliams walked around the side of the store where Dalton had found the cigarette butts. He saw Katie Mae smoking at the corner behind the building.

"Starting a habit?"

Katie Mae turned. "Of talking to you? All right."

He grinned, walked over to her. "Glad to see you. Had a question."

"All right."

"The two guys who came in here. You sure you'd never seen them before?"

"Not in those masks," she said.

"Think about the eyes. Think about those eyes on a different face."

"Okay."

"What color were the eyes?"

"Which guy?"

"Either?"

"The tall one?" Katie Mae said. She hadn't said anything about height before. Said they were both normal build. Normal everything. Except for the accents and the masks. And the pistols.

"Sure," McWilliams said. "The one taller than me?"

"About your height, I guess. He had green eyes. Like brown green."

"And the other one?"

"Brown."

"Dark brown?"

"I don't know," she said, the moment gone. "Just brown. Hey, Daddy said you used to be a pitcher. Like played in the big leagues and all."

McWilliams leaned against the wall. "I used to pitch. Long time ago."

"I'm a pitcher, too. Think you could show me some stuff?"

"Afraid I don't know much about softball."

"Softball, shit," she said. "Two-time All-Star with the Tigers. Trying out for the team as soon as I can."

"Which team? High school?"

"Yeah. Think you can help me?"

He laughed. "Glad to, your daddy say it's fine."

"I got a hellacious fastball. You better be ready."

"Yeah, well, a good fastball doesn't mean too much."

"Daddy said you threw 100 miles an hour."

"Not hardly," he said. "Don't focus on the speed. It ain't about how fast you get there. It's about where you get. About where the batter thinks you're going to get."

"Yeah?"

"It's about setting something up. Getting the guy to lean outside early in the count and then jamming him tight."

"Well, I can pitch strikes all day long."

"That's what I'm talking about," McWilliams said. He hadn't talked baseball in, hell, years really, but he fell right back in. Muscle memory. The way you miss time with a leg injury and work your way back. Then how your arm finds the slot, the release point. How there's that moment when you stop thinking about your hips and your shoulder and your elbow angle. How all those pieces just come together and you stop thinking. And you don't even realize it. You just throw. "It's not about strikes. It's about knowing the situation."

"What do you mean?"

"Like you've got one out, tight ball game, and the guy at bat has three balls and no strikes. And he's a power hitter. What do you do?"

"Tight game? Keep him off the bases. Like you said. Pitch him, get him leaning out, jam him in. Paint the black."

"No, not even the black. You keep the ball clear of the plate. He's a power hitter. This guy is slow. And the guy coming up next is the catcher."

"I ain't afraid. I'll throw it right past him. Country hardball."

"Then he hits it out of the park. Bad guys win. Drive home safely."

"What am I supposed to do?"

"You walk him. Let him get to first. Then pitch the next guy inside for a ground ball to the shortstop. Double play ball."

"Yeah. I've seen them do that."

"Sometimes you break out the country hardball, but sometimes you let them hit it. You just have to be ready when they do."

"Won't that walk look bad on your stats?"

"You can't worry about that. You sacrifice that. Hell, we were playing El Dorado one year and I walked a guy with the bases loaded. Gave up a run to get to the next batter. Start with a clean slate. No balls. No strikes. And I went after him. But I had to give up that one run to get to him. To pitch him inside."

"What happened?"

"I hit him in the head."

"Holy shit."

"Yeah, but the next one flied out to second and I struck the next guy out. We scored four runs next time up. Won that by something like three runs, I think. It's all in knowing the situation. Being willing to give something up when you have to. It's not always about fastballs down the middle."

He heard the car door open behind him and turned to see Caskey waiting.

When they got back on the road, Caskey asked about Gene. "You think he was trying to tip us off? Make sure we didn't get hurt?"

"No."

"Well?" Caskey waited. "Well what, then?"

"I think he was trying to set us up."

"How do you mean? Like get us killed?"

"Shot at. Probably not killed."

"No shit?" Caskey hummed a little. "Damn. That's messed up."

"Yeah."

"So, why you think that?"

"Because he works for Rudd. And Rudd needs someone to blame this on."

"Someone to take the rap?"

Jesus Christ. "Yeah." McWilliams looked over, saw Caskey biting his lip and nodding, the wheels spinning like wet tires in loose gravel.

"So how was he going to do that?"

"It's a big place. Remember a few years back, those hunters found a field of pot on his farm?"

"Oh, yeah. And he said some worker did that? Some Mexicans he had?"

"Yeah. And the place was so big, he couldn't be expected to know what happened on every inch every day."

"Those Mexicans got deported, didn't they?"

"Probably."

"So someone was going to start shooting at us when we got into the barn?"

"Yeah. And Gene wanted us to know for sure that Rudd didn't have anything to do with it. Guy's already setting up court testimony and he isn't even arrested yet."

"So then what?"

"The barn?"

Caskey nodded.

"I don't know," McWilliams said. "Maybe he told one of the workers to shoot near the cops, then give up and take the blame.

Said he'd get him a good lawyer, get his family some money. And maybe Gene warned us," McWilliams tapped his fingers on the dash, thinking quickly, "maybe Gene warned us so we'd know what was coming. Maybe Rudd was hoping we'd take the shooter out and he could blame everything on the dead guy."

"Damn, that's a great plan."

"Yeah. No telling. Calling the guy out and finding all that pot in the barn means Rudd's going to have a lot of court dates coming up."

"So how come today? Why this time? It's like you knew we were going to find it."

"Yeah. That's because of the hat."

"The toboggan?"

"Yeah. That made it a search warrant for a robbery."

"So? Still found the pot. And didn't find anything about the robbery."

"Right. Because the whole thing was a setup."

"What whole thing?"

"The robbery," McWilliams said, leaning his head on the headrest.

"How do you mean?"

"Two guys rob the place. Then the only evidence pops up at the end of Rudd's driveway? On a public road?"

"Whoa. No kidding. Whoever robbed the store wanted to frame Rudd."

"Not frame Rudd. They wanted his place searched. Draw us out there so we'd find the whole damn operation."

Caskey nodded, thought about it. "But why now? How did they know there'd be all that shit there today?"

"Who signed off on the search warrant?"

"Judge Gordon."

"How is that different than all the other warrants?"

"Because this time we found something?"

"No." McWilliams squeezed his eyes shut, took a breath. "Because this one didn't go through the multijurisdictional grand jury because it was for a store robbery, not a drug search."

"Holy shit."

"Yeah."

"So you think Judge Boggs was tipping off Rudd before? Saying here comes the search?"

"I don't think anything. I'm just noticing some things. Some inconsistencies."

"It has to be Boggs."

"No, could be someone in his office."

"I guess," Caskey said. He whistled. "Damn. Somebody's going to be in a world of hurt." They pulled into the parking lot for the sheriff's office. "Hey, what about the cigarettes? What about that?"

McWilliams thumbed the pack in his pocket. "Guess that turned out to be nothing," he said.

✦ ✦ ✦

On the way to Grady and Delsie's that night, McWilliams asked Cora about her brother's employment.

"He's doing some odd jobs, I think. Delsie's doing all right with the beauty shop, she told me. He'll find something."

"Good."

"I know why you're asking."

"Just asking."

"You think he's going to get mixed up in all that nonsense you think he was mixed up in before."

McWilliams didn't say anything.

"You still think he's some kind of criminal ring leader. You need to let that go. Dennis, he's my brother. You think I don't know him?"

"I was just asking."

"All right. Fine. Look, I don't want to go through all this again. It's over and done with, and I don't want you to keep bringing it up."

"I wasn't. Just asking about the job search."

"Well, don't mention anything about it tonight. You can say something about the beauty shop. That would be nice. But don't say anything about Grady not finding work. He's touchy about that. You men always are."

"All right."

"Let's not fight. I don't want to fight about this. Let's just have a nice, quiet evening with no trouble. You turn off your radio and your cell?"

"You know I can't do that."

"Oh, right. You men and your jobs."

McWilliams didn't say anything.

"I'm sorry, sweetie," she said, putting her hand on his leg. "But he's my brother. And I don't want to talk about it."

"I know," McWilliams said, holding her hand.

When they pulled up at the house, he asked Cora to go on in and send Grady out. Wanted to show him a problem with the truck's engine.

"Howdy, deputy," Grady said as he walked down the steps to McWilliams. "Cora said you're having some engine trouble. What's the problem?"

"Oh, it's probably nothing," he said, closing the hood of his truck. "You hear about all the commotion up at Rudd's farm today? Big day."

"Commotion?" Grady rubbed his chin, looked away to nothing. "No, can't say as I did. They have a fire?"

"Found a bunch of drugs up there. Grass in the barn. Meth lab in the old slaves' house. All sorts of trouble."

"Hunh. You don't say." Grady kicked the gravel at his feet.

"Yeah. Sounds like he's out of business for a while."

"Well, I guess you'll be out of a job. No more potheads to bust."

"Still got a few folks here and there. And you remember Clay Sawyer. He's still in business. Wasn't he a friend of yours?"

"I don't know about him. That was all a long time ago," Grady said. "I haven't seen him in, well, I don't know. Long time."

"That right?"

"Yeah. You ready to go back in? I think the girls wanted to eat a quick dinner and play some cards." Grady scratched the back of his neck, turned to the house.

"In a second," McWilliams said. "Just need a quick smoke."

"When did you start smoking again?"

"Oh, you know, job's stressful right now," McWilliams said, pulling the pack out of his pocket and offering one to Grady.

"I'm trying to give that up," Grady said. He looked down at the pack. "Hey, Carolina Select. That's my brand."

PRODIGAL

Hank Dalton was dragging his index finger down the morning's sports page. This was after supper on a Tuesday, box scores had been reprinted from Monday's paper. So he was scrolling through Sunday's games, recreating what he could. A couple of days behind, which was just fine. No rush.

The kid from Magnolia, the Womacks' boy, had gotten into the game against the Padres. Pinch-hitting for the pitcher. One at-bat. Nothing to show for it. Padres over the Marlins. "Hope he went down swinging."

"What's that?" Ruby asked from across the den, looking up from her crossword.

"Oh, nothing," he said. "Just mumbling to myself."

She moved an afghan, patted the couch. Took off her drugstore reading glasses. Set them on the side table. "Well, come mumble a little to me."

When he got up to move closer, he heard the gravel pop on the edge of the road in front of their house. A car going slowly along.

He walked to the front windows, spread the curtains. The sun was dropping to the tree line in the field across the way, the slowing car in darkness, then light. Shadows inside.

"Who's out there?" she asked. "We got company?"

"No. Just looks like someone's having a bad day."

"Well, I hope it isn't company," she said. "We could use a little quiet around here."

He nodded. Took a breath. "I'll see what the trouble is, if they need something," Hank said, letting the screen door close behind him as he stood on the front steps.

"Just be careful," Ruby called after him.

But he wasn't paying attention to his wife just then. His full attention was devoted to the man now standing next to him, the man with the pistol pressing under Hank's jaw, the man in the ski mask, pressing his mouth against Hank's ear and saying "motherfucker" this and "motherfucker" that.

Hank should have known to be careful.

About two weeks before, sixteen days to be exact, he and Ruby had walked through their side door to find their house had been robbed. The night had been perfect until then. They'd gotten the good news from Ruby's oncologist and called a few people to celebrate. By the time they got from the clinic in Texarkana to Wiley's on the Bayou, three dozen people had joined in the full-remission party. Bernice had to set aside the meeting room for them, bumping the Rotary meeting to a few tables by the kitchen. No one complained. In fact, the Rotarians came along, too, all so pleased as hell Hank's wife was going to be all right. No, you never know, but this is great news. The Good Lord is looking after ya, Hank. Luck's coming around, yes, sir. She's the strongest woman I ever did see. Everyone shaking hands, hugging. Most of them wondering the same thing.

Someone must have called Chet.

Wouldn't Hank and Ruby have called? Your mother gets this kind of news, doesn't the family call? Were we supposed to call?

Hell, you know how Chet is. He's probably too doped up to move.

Don't say that. Don't you talk like that tonight. Of all nights. Don't you talk like that about their son.

I'm not saying anything you weren't thinking.

Well, just don't say it. Not tonight.

All right.

A couple of the men, after enough congratulatory time had passed, came over to talk to Hank. Away from the women.

"Great news, Hank."

"Great news."

"Yeah," Hank said. "Not out of the woods, yet, I don't guess. Never are, really."

"My wife's brother had cancer off and on for ten years," Eddie Pribble said. "Went to chemo. Radiation. Went to the little Chinese fellow over in El Dorado. Stuck needles all up and down his back. In his arm. Did everything they could think of. Took 'em damn near a decade, but they got his ass cancer free."

"What kind of cancer did he have?" one of the men asked.

"Like I said, butthole cancer."

The men groaned, looked somewhere else.

"He wasn't gay or nothing like that," Pribble said. "Just caught it in the a-hole, somehow."

They all said "damn" and shook their heads. You just never know.

"He doing all right now?" Hank asked.

"Naw. Lost his job. All the medical bills. Sick days. Took a shotgun to his head last Easter. Blew his jaw into a hundred pieces, clear across the kitchen. Earlene and the girl moved to Vicksburg. She works at that big Chinese buffet off the interstate. Nice place."

The smell of fried fish was dying off. Squeaks and chirps coming in off the water. Catfish, frogs, something flopping here and there on the water.

"Damned shame. I think I remember something about that last year," somebody said.

"Yeah," Pribble said. "It was in the paper."

On the way home, Hank and Ruby held hands, awkwardly, across the emergency brake between them. But neither one let go until they pulled up the drive. He pulled her hand to his, gave hers a kiss, then put the Jeep in park, took the keys out, walked across the carport to the side door, and saw through the window the mess inside.

She walked in, said "sweet Jesus" the way you might start a prayer. Then they walked through the house, seeing what was missing. Neither of them gave any thought to whether someone else was still in the house. They called the sheriff's office and started making a list of what was missing. Then they sat at the kitchen table, drank coffee, waited.

"So that's it?" Deputy Lacewell asked. "They came right for the safe?"

"Far as we can tell," Hank said, standing in the bedroom with the deputy. "Made a mess of the place, but didn't take anything else. Pistol and some money from the safe."

"How much money you say it was?"

"Didn't say."

"Well," Lacewell said, moving his tongue around the back of his teeth. "How much was it?"

"You need me to say?"

"I'm asking you."

"I mean, what's the point. It's cash. It's gone. Not like I had the serial numbers written down. Can't you just put 'Stolen: Cash'?"

"Was it a lot of cash?" Lacewell asked.

"Enough to take, I reckon."

"Hank, I get the feeling you're not being completely forthright with me."

He nodded. "Yeah, I'd say that's a fair assessment."

"Well?" Lacewell waited.

"What if I told you it was twenty-two thousand dollars?"

"Jesus H. Christ, Hank," he said, catching Ruby's attention from the living room. "Sorry, ma'am." He nodded her way. He lowered his voice. "Shit, Hank, that's a fucking shitload of money. What you got that much cash for? Holy Christ."

"I'm just saying, what if I told you that's how much?"

The deputy shook his head. "I'd tell you that's a lot of damn money to have lying around the house and I'd ask you why the hell you had that kind of cash."

"What if I said I'm not a fan of banks?"

"I'd want to know why you had that kind of cash. Jesus, Hank. This is starting to sound a little questionable, if you don't mind my saying."

"I mean, that's something you'd have to put in the report, the amount of cash."

"Yeah, I'd sure as hell think so," Lacewell said.

Deputy Dennis McWilliams had come over from talking to Ruby. He'd talked to her about the doctor's visit, heard the good news. Said they were all praying for her. In the bedroom, he asked Lacewell what was going on.

Once he was caught up, he looked at Hank. Then he scratched the back of his neck. "So you had two thousand dollars?"

"Is that what I had?" Hank asked him, then looked to Lacewell.

"I'm not sure that's what he said."

McWilliams turned to Lacewell. "Mike, how about you make sure Mrs. Dalton's all right, okay? Been a long day for her. Maybe she'd like a glass of water." He took Lacewell's notebook, pulled the last page out, slid it into his pocket, and handed the notebook back.

When Dalton and McWilliams were alone, the deputy said, "My dad wasn't a fan of banks, either."

"That right?"

"Said he didn't need the feds breathing down his neck about how much money he made and how much he had to pay in taxes, you know?"

"Yeah."

"Guess he figured the shoebox under his mattress was his Cayman Islands account."

"That sounds like a smart man."

McWilliams nodded. "It was good money. He was just kinda particular about who got a piece of it."

Hank nodded. "Smart man, indeed."

"And the combination to the lock?"

"Yeah?" Hank asked. "What do you mean?"

"Anniversary? Phone number? Your kids' birthdays?" McWilliams asked, wincing after he said it.

Hank nodded. "Birthdays and mine and Ruby's anniversary."

"When's the last time you changed it?"

"When the guy put it in."

McWilliams looked around the bed. "Still a little peculiar they just came straight for the cash."

"And the pistol."

"Yeah." McWilliams looked at the registration Hank had handed him. "A .32, huh?"

"A Colt, right."

"No other guns in the house."

"No," Hank said. Not since their firstborn, Billy, had died in that hunting accident over around Lewisville six years ago. The sort of day you play through with "what ifs" for the rest of your life. No. A pistol to keep the house safe was all. No rifles. No one was doing any hunting anymore.

"And they didn't take anything else?"

"Not much for them to take, don't reckon."

"TV? Computer? Jewelry?"

"Old. No. And cheap. Ruby has a diamond necklace, but it's her good luck charm. She was wearing it today. Probably still is."

"All right." McWilliams held the registration between his fingers. "Might want to see about getting another pistol."

Hank nodded, but never got around to getting one. Not that it would have helped him sixteen days later when the man on his steps was holding a pistol on him.

The man with Hank waited as his partner pulled the car next to the carport, got out of the car, pulled a shotgun from the back seat. The man with the shotgun said, "Get inside."

Hank came through the door first, and Ruby asked what was going on. Then she saw the two men behind him. She had taken her slippers off while he was outside, was scrolling through the channels to find something to watch.

"Get your asses down on the ground," the man with the shotgun said.

Hank went to one knee, all creaks and pops. He looked over at Ruby, thinking to reassure her. Ruby didn't move.

The man with the shotgun stepped her way.

"Get your ass down on the ground, bitch."

Hank started to say something, but Ruby stood from the couch, holding the afghan tight in her hand. "The hell I will."

The three men looked at her.

"What?"

"I done beat cancer," she said, "and I swear to God I ain't getting down on the ground for nobody."

The gunmen looked at each other, then back at Ruby.

The sun painted light onto the rug in front of her feet, as flecks of dust danced in a river to the window, every speck visible, sparkling, like your first glimpse of snow. The dust, caught for a moment, before the sun goes away and the dust settles, moving by books, by afghans, by the top edge of a picture frame, from room to room in the darkness.

When the man with the pistol moved from Hank to Ruby, Hank uncoiled, putting his shoulder into the man's gun.

A thin, piercing sound as a shot exploded into the wall. The man with the shotgun turned back, but the gun barrels hit the other man in the shoulder and two blasts discharged pellets into a cabinet of family photos. The Sears family photo of the Daltons in front. Hank in his funeral suit. Ruby with a fresh perm. Billy and Chet, standing as tall as they could. A decade old. A lifetime ago.

Hank fought for the pistol, managed to put another shot into the wall. The men ran out the way they'd come, gravel spraying as they tore off. Hank and Ruby in the living room, holding each other.

He held his left hand open for her. "Got my gun back."

"That's your gun?"

"Yeah."

He set it on the cabinet top, winced as he moved.

"What's wrong?"

He put his left hand on his right collarbone. "Think I broke my shoulder."

Hank Dalton pulled his truck into his son's driveway, cut the engine. He squeezed the steering wheel. Let go. Squeezed again.

He had spent the early afternoon listening to the ball game, Justin Womack getting in the game because the regular second baseman had pulled a hammy running out a grounder. Justin had gotten an RBI double in the eighth to tie the game, then scored the winning run on a wild pitch.

"Did you hear that?" Hank asked Ruby.

"Very nice."

"You weren't paying attention?"

"Sure," she said, looking up from her crossword. "Sure. That was amazing."

"Really?"

"Okay. I didn't hear it," she grinned. "What was it?"

He told her, taking three times as long to tell it as it had taken to play out.

"Justin. He's Chet's age, right?"

"Year older." The year between Chet and Billy.

As Hank stood from his car, looking at his son's little house, he replayed parts of the game in his head, still trying to put good thoughts on top of bad ones.

It wasn't much of a driveway. Enough for a car and a half, maybe. He started to close the door with his slinged arm, shoulder stinging. Sneered, used the other arm. The old house was so close to the road, when something fell off, it'd as likely flop right into the road as anywhere, he figured, walking through the side yard, heading around back. He stood at the foot of the steps, plywood on milk crates, looking around the back yard, littered with lawn mowers, metal chairs, truck tires.

He walked through the back, caught the screen door before it could slam shut, eased it closed. He touched the bottoms of his boots to the rug, dried the dampness. Then walked through the mudroom into the kitchen, past the brown jugs on the floor, the burners on the counter, the empty drugstore boxes.

The house was empty, except for loose CDs, ash-topped beer cans, a bong as long as a baseball bat, and the boy sleeping on the yard-sale couch. He looked at what was left of the boy, skin tight over points of bone. A sprawling, dull tattoo on his chest, never finished. Maybe it was supposed to have been a dragon. Or smoke.

He stood over the boy, watching him sleep. There was a time he was faster than the Womack boy. Stronger than his own older brother. The promise. The absolute, complete hope.

Once, when he was a high school sophomore, the boy had one-hopped a throw from the wall in right field, nailing what would have been the tying run from third. They'd gone to state after that, Hank and Ruby driving to every game, setting up lawn chairs early, bringing food and drinks from the store, making sure the whole team was all right. And that championship game, when even Billy had skipped class to see Chet play, everyone standing for the last three innings. Everyone storming the field after the boy's walk-off solo shot in the eleventh. So much promise. So close to home.

And then the hunting accident, like an earthquake. Or fire. Like a flood that sweeps over everything, soaking ruin into everything, until years later even the box of family photographs you'd thought was tucked away safe in the attic still reeks of mildew.

Hank kicked the couch to wake the boy. Then again.

The boy wiped his nose with his forearm. "C'mon. The hell?" He saw his father, reached for a shirt that wasn't there. "Dad." He blinked, shook his head. Started to cough up something, then swallowed it.

"Afternoon," Hank said.

Chet looked around. "You can't just come in my house while I'm sleeping. What are you doing here?" He slid up to sit on the couch, looking around the room, trying to see where things lay.

Hank turned his back on the boy, walked around the room. "Came to check on you. Make sure you were safe."

"Safe?" Chet scratched the back of head. "Yeah. Wait. Why wouldn't I be safe?"

"Been a lot of break-ins around here," Hank said. "I notice here you got a nice big-screen TV now. Work going all right?"

"Uh, yeah. Work's fine."

"Where you working?"

"Oh, you know."

Hank turned to face his son. "No. I don't know."

"Around."

"That right? And what are you doing?"

"You know, this and that."

"Yeah. I know about this and that. Must pay well."

"I'm doing all right."

Hank reached for the Colt from inside his sling. He pointed the pistol at the TV. "What is that? Forty-six inches?"

"Hey, hey. Careful, man."

"The TV? Forty-six inches?" Hank shook the pistol toward the TV again.

"Forty-two I think. Hell. Be careful."

The blast echoed as Hank sent a shattering hole through the center of the TV. He looked at the boy's reflection in the edge of the screen. The ghost of the young boy. The boy he'd let—what was the term? Slip away? Fall apart? Drift? But this was the moment. He had hoped that at some time the boy would come back, like the prodigal son. Saying he had been lost, but he wanted to come home. And they would have a party, like in the story. And everything from the past few years would be like that, stories to tell. And Hank would know that he'd saved his son. That the promise hadn't been lost, that he was right to have left the boy alone to find his own way. He'd been lost in the woods, but had found his way back. Like in the book Brother Obie had brought Ruby after the accident. How you cope with tragedy by becoming stronger in your faith. Now, bringing Chet back to the family, before he wandered too far away.

"Jesus Christ," the boy said as parts of the TV flaked away, dropped like crystals into the dust. He got to his feet, moved toward his father.

Hank turned the pistol on the boy. "How much and who?"

"What?"

"Not what. Sit down."

The boy sat.

"How much do you owe? Who do you owe?"

The boy lifted his chin, looked away, snorted. "I don't owe nobody shit. I'm Chet fucking Dalton."

"Yeah," his father sighed. "I know."

MIRACLES

"I'm sorry for your loss. I'm sorry for your loss," he whispered. Hands in his pants pockets, he slid his thumbs into his fists, squeezed until his knuckles ached. "I'm sorry for your loss."

The man in front of him turned around, lifted his glasses to his forehead. "What was that?"

"Nothing. Sorry." Rusty swallowed, felt his Adam's apple jump, tight against his collar, against the clip of his tie.

The man turned away as Jake slid in next to him, punched him in the shoulder. "Dude, 'sup?"

Rusty didn't turn. He looked at the back of the man in front of him, the white edge of the man's shirt collar, a knife-edge standing a quarter inch above his jacket collar. Over the man's shoulder, Rusty saw the line snaking through the hall, imagined it as it turned between the pews, to the front of the sanctuary where Staci McMahen's family stood, squeezing hugs into cries.

The church was quiet now, a dull murmur, after the deputies escorted F. T. Pribble out.

"Is that . . . ?" a woman had asked when Pribble walked in from the parking lot. Rusty had been in line long enough that a dozen people were behind him when Deputy McWilliams walked Pribble back outside.

147

"I understand," Rusty had heard him say. "I just come to pay my respects, say I was sorry for what my family done."

When the deputy walked back into the church, everyone in line turned forward, watching the back of the person ahead of them.

Someone said, "Lot of nerve."

Jake leaned in to Rusty's face, shaking Rusty from the whispers. "Bet they ain't got this many people when you die."

"Shh," Rusty said.

"Hey, kid," said a man two or three people behind them. Rusty turned, saw a man he recognized but didn't know. "You can't cut. Back of the line."

Jake looked at the man for a few seconds. "See you after," he said to Rusty. Then he turned, walked away.

Rusty let him go, then stood on his toes, trying to count the people ahead of him, measure the time in handshakes, in hugs. He turned to the woman behind him, a woman his mother knew. "I'll be right back, okay?"

When she nodded, he walked toward the front of the line, to where it turned through the double doors, cross handles bungeed to the railing, and counted again, in clumps of ten. There's four, then five, six. Maybe a dozen, fifteen groups of ten lined up, waiting to be sorry for their loss. Rusty wiped his forehead with the sleeve of his shirt, then pulled the handkerchief from his pocket, wiped the damp from his cheeks. People come for the show. People coming into church like they always do. Put on a tie. Act like you're friends with everyone.

How many of these people even knew Staci? Rusty saw Debbie. Tina. Loriella. A girl whose name he didn't know. How many knew who she really was? Talked with her about anything real? Shared something with her. How many of these people had any right to be there at all?

He walked back to the woman, told her again that he'd be right back, then walked outside the church.

Rusty leaned against the brick wall, under the canopy they'd built a few years before for rainy-day drop-offs. He watched as cars pulled into the parking lot, circled through the trucks and suburbans, then pulled back onto the road and into the Methodists' parking lot across the street. All the people who came in all the cars. Why Staci? Why not one of them? Rusty saw a man in the front row, sitting in a station wagon, head leaned back, hands on the steering wheel, patting time to a song Rusty couldn't hear. A few spots away, F. T. Pribble sat on his tailgate, legs dangling, pants legs creeping up against bone-white legs.

Rusty saw a man in a tan suit walk up the sidewalk from the back of the church. The wind was blowing a little, pine needles falling into the road as the man walked.

"Afternoon, son," the man said, tipping his straw hat to Rusty. "You look lost."

Rusty turned behind him, wondered why the man was talking to him. "No, sir. Just had to get some air or whatever."

The man nodded. "Mind if I sit with you for a bit?"

"Free country, I guess."

The man sat down on the curb. "Name's Obadiah Roberson. Everybody calls me Brother Obie, though."

"I'm Rusty. That's what everybody calls me."

"Well, Rusty, I expect there's a big turnout today."

"Yes, sir. Guess so."

"You family? Friend?"

"I go to school with Staci. Went to school, I mean."

The old man looked off at the needles blowing down from the trees, dark-tipped clumps spiraling down, propeller-like into the gravel.

"She was a good person," Brother Obie said.

"How do you know that?" Rusty blurted out. "You didn't know her. I don't even know who you are."

"I hadn't seen the family in a decade, but they're good people."

Rusty squinted, then cocked his head and nodded. "Hey, I remember you. You used to be the preacher here."

"Not for a while."

"You quit?"

"The Lord has use of me elsewhere."

"Wish he had use for me elsewhere," Rusty said.

"And why is that?"

"Look around, man. This place sucks."

"All God's world," Brother Obie said.

"And where was God when Staci needed Him?"

Brother Obie didn't say anything.

"I mean," Rusty said, "I been thinking, right? The Lord works in mysterious ways. The Lord never gives you more than you can handle. My mom's been saying that for the past week, and now you go how it's God's world. Well, if it's his world, how about a miracle now and then, right?"

"A miracle?"

A car pulled up beside the two of them. Ken Moody rolled down his windows. "You fellas okay? Need a lift?" They shook their heads and he waved, drove on.

"How about it?" Rusty asked. "How come God couldn't save her?"

"What would you have the Almighty do, son?"

"I don't know. Walk on water. Raise the dead. How come God only did stuff like that in the Bible? Why can't he help people now?"

"You think the Lord doesn't help people now?"

"He didn't help Staci, did he? Nobody did. Nobody ever helps anybody around here."

Brother Obie reached into his jacket pocket, pulled out a pack of cigarettes. Took one and offered the pack to Rusty. Rusty shook his head. Obie lit one, put the pack back into his jacket. "You mention walking on water. So you're familiar with the story?"

"Yeah. They're all out on the boat and Jesus walks on the water and they all freak out."

"Like a magic trick?"

"Yeah. Exactly."

"You know, in the Gospel of Thomas, right after Jesus walks on the water and heals a leper, he saws Mary Magdalene in half."

Rusty laughed. "I think you might be making that up."

"That's why the Council of Trent voted that one out of the canon. Pope Paul the Third hated magicians."

"You're nuts."

"But they left the lion pulling the rabbit out of the hat in Revelations. That's just good, clean fun."

"All right. Now I know you're making it up."

"How do you know that?"

"Rabbit out of a hat? Sawing a lady in half?"

"Is that crazier than walking on the water? Getting wine from a pitcher of water? Feeding thousands of people with a couple of fish?"

"You telling me the Bible is made up?"

"No, son. Just that you're reading it wrong."

"What do you mean?"

"You asked me why didn't God do what you wanted."

"No, I didn't."

"You did. You wanted him to, what did you say, 'save' Staci McMahen. You wanted that, and you asked why God didn't do what you wanted."

"I didn't mean he should save her because of me. I meant he should save her because, you know, because of her. A good person. Like why would God let that happen to her? To Staci?"

"Let me tell you about Jesus walking on the water, Rusty."

"I know the story already."

"No, you don't. Jesus and his followers were at the fishing village of Bethsaida. The Son of Man had been teaching to the crowds, feeding the multitude with two fish and some bread, and at the end of the day, he climbed a mountain, away from everyone, to pray. The disciples went back to the boat for the evening. In the middle of the night, the boat had drifted far from shore and the disciples onboard were struggling against the storm, the waves. They looked up and Jesus came walking across the water, climbed into the boat, and said, 'It's me. Have a little faith.' See, they had thought he was a ghost. Then they floated across the water and all the people in the towns wheeled out their sick for the Son of Man to heal."

Rusty nodded. "All right. Longer than what I said, but same thing."

"The story is about faith, son. About the calm in the storm." Obie took a long drag from his cigarette, tried blowing rings into the air.

"You saying trust in Jesus? How does that bring Staci back? I'm saying why can't we have a miracle now? Jesus does a thousand miracles a year back before videotape, and now he won't do any?"

"Rusty, do you know where Bethsaida is?"

"Where Jesus walked on water?"

"Right."

"In the Bible, I guess. I don't know."

Obie turned up the heel of his shoe, crushed out the cigarette, and put the butt into his pants pocket. "No one knows for certain. See, there are camps set up on either side. Bethsaida Julius, east

152

of the Jordan River. And then there's Bethsaida Galilee, which is where four or five of the disciples were from. You see, 'Bethsaida' means 'fishing village,' so there could have been more than one place."

"So what?"

"Well, if this is where Jesus walked on water, where he fed thousands with two fish, then wouldn't you like to have a jar of sand from here? Maybe you could sprinkle it on your arm if it breaks. Use it to perform miracles."

"I don't think it works like that," Rusty said. "So what does it matter?"

"Oh, it matters a great deal. You have scholars and believers arguing one Bethsaida, two Bethsaidas. It matters a great deal to them."

"I guess."

"See, Rusty, they are like the townspeople who brought out their dead and dying. They want the Son of Man to perform miracles. Magic tricks. And these matter a great deal to them. To these people, Jesus Christ was a traveling magician, walking on water, making the blind see. He was a miracle man."

"I know. That's what I'm saying. He could pop into the church right now and raise the dead. So why won't he help her? Why can't he save her?"

"I could tell you the Lord works in mysterious ways. I could tell you that the Devil brings wickedness upon us all. But that isn't what matters right now. This is not a logic exam, son. This is the day that Staci McMahen's family grieves for their loss, for the darkness that extinguished a light. And this is the day for faith. It doesn't matter how many Bethsaidas there are or whether Jesus walked across the water. The miracle isn't the number of fish he had. The miracle is the feeding. Don't worry about the walking on the water, son. Focus on getting in the boat." Brother Obie stood, dusted the back of his pants. "Reckon you ought to get back inside, don't you?"

"I don't know what to say."

"You knew Staci, didn't you?"

"Yeah. The last night, I mean, when she went missing, that night she was talking to me about stars. How they're close together but the closer you get, how they get farther away."

"You miss her?"

"Yeah."

"Tell them that. Get in the boat with them. Have a little faith."

Rusty was standing at the front doors of the sanctuary, thinking about what Brother Obie had said. Have faith. Belief. Trust. Close your eyes and pray. Give yourself over. Rusty closed his eyes, pictured himself and Staci back at school. Pictured that day when the Red Cross came to the school, everyone laid out on the lawn chairs in the teachers' lounge, blood easing through the tubes. His friends eating Little Debbies from a tray. Taking the "Give Blood" T-shirts from the box. And Staci talking to one of the women there about blood and needles and the woman calling it "life's liquid." And how Staci had said she wanted to be a doctor after that and he'd talked to her about the pre-calc class coming up. And how she'd written that half-page note in his yearbook. Not something about how it's been great to be in class with you or you'll go far. But a real note about how much it meant to her that he'd helped her with the math. Like, how much he had meant to her, he thought. And then he thought about how the girl who wrote that note to him, who'd laughed when he'd told her the first derivative of a cow was prime rib, how he'd never be with her. Not ever again.

He heard a clanging thump from the parking lot. He turned, saw Mr. Pribble's legs poking out of the back of his truck.

He walked to the truck, saw F. T. Pribble staring up at the sky. Pribble turned his head. "You one of the girl's classmates?"

Rusty turned around, wondering if the deputy was still inside. "I was. Yes, sir. You okay?"

"They don't want me inside there."

Rusty looked around for help, for someone else. "No."

"Can't say as I blame them."

"No."

"You see how clear the sky is?" Pribble asked. "How empty?"

"Yes, sir."

"I might have had a little to drink today."

"Okay. I need to get back inside."

"I just wanted to say something to them. The people on the inside," Pribble said. "Just, I don't know."

Rusty looked up at the thin blue sky. "You sure that isn't a star there?" He pointed.

"That's an airplane, kid. All by its lonesome."

Behind him was a sanctuary of people. People with jobs and cars and guns and houses. A multitude of people. And there would be more. There would always be more, coming together. The funerals. The fundraising concerts. The church service. People putting on their suits. People standing inside the building, talking about faith and hope and charity. People talking about miracles.

In the sanctuary, Staci McMahen was gone, face up to the sky while the unconnected people around her walked, one step at a time, to frown at her parents on the way to dinner at Wiley's, gas at the mini-mart.

The moment with Staci, that moment in the field when everything was clear, when for just that blinking second everything made sense, that was gone, too.

Rusty stepped up into the bed of the truck, sat down on a tackle box. "Mind if I join you?"

"Suit yourself." Pribble sat up, leaned against the back of the truck. "Tackle box. Slide that over, will ya?"

Rusty hunched up, pushed the box along, sat down in the bed of the truck.

Pribble pulled out what was left of an Early Times pint, drank down through the backwash. "Good shit," he said, closed his eyes. "I just wanted to say something to them," he said. "Say how bad it was. How it's all this spread all over all of us, right? How it's like this cloud, like how it's come down, right? On us all." He looked around the bed of the truck, searching for something. Coughed something over the side of the truck and leaned back again. "Can't nobody even say anything. You say you're sorry for what happened, they think it's your fault, you know? Like the one who does that, apology, the one who gives the apology, I'm saying." He shook his head, snorted. "They say that's the one who ought to be sorry, right? Like that's the person who has the fault of the thing, right?"

Rusty nodded, looked to the church.

"Yeah. You best go on back in there," Pribble said. "'Cause they're the only ones anything ever happened to. 'Cause it's them, right? Everybody wants them to feel better. What about my brother? He's got two dead boys 'cause of what happened. 'Cause of what they done. But my brother didn't do anything. I didn't do anything. Right?"

Rusty nodded.

"Right?" Pribble shouted this time, leaning forward. "God-damn right, right. Anybody ever give a shit about us? Ever? No. Didn't nobody ever do shit."

Pribble put an arm on the edge of the truck and Rusty watched the empty bottle arc through the air, across the parking lot, tiny points of light along glass corners as it flew further away. The bottle reached as high as it could, then came down quicker, thumping into a flowerbed near the sidewalk where no one would notice it.

Rusty eased out of the bed of the truck, watching Pribble as he snorted, blinked, started to fade away. The boy stepped to the ground, lifted the tailgate until it latched shut. "Mr. Pribble," he said.

F. T. Pribble lifted an eyebrow, opened an eye.

Rusty put his hands on the top of the tailgate. "I'm sorry for your loss," he said, and walked back to the church.

HARVEST

PART ONE

I put down the tray of deviled eggs, minus the three I'd just eaten, at the end of the church's homecoming picnic table.

"Are you trying to get in trouble?" A woman's voice from behind me.

I turned to see a dark-haired woman in a yellow T-shirt, jeans, and a pair of blue sneakers. She was about my age, grinning at me. I found a plastic fork, stabbed another deviled egg, and handed it to her. "They're my grandmother's. You should try one."

She took the fork out of my hand. "No, you're putting those in the desserts." She ate the egg and handed me the fork. "Those go up that way." She nodded toward the church, at the other end of two fifty-yard-long tables.

My grandmother was up by the church, talking to people I used to know. Cousins of some sort, mostly. Small talk. Gossip. Did you hear about so-and-so? The sort of nothing we use to fill the emptiness between waking up and going to sleep.

Lawn chairs were clicking open around the church, filling the field and the gravel parking lot for the homecoming lunch. Long, wood-planked tables under dying oak trees. Cardboard boxes lined with foil, piled with fried chicken. Clear bowls of salads, layered with beans and cheese. Pots of turnip greens with chunks of bacon and potato. Silver trays of mac and cheese. Black-eyed peas. Chocolate cakes with damp icing and pies with six-inch meringues. And me with a tray of deviled eggs at the wrong end of everything.

I ate another egg.

A little bit of relish. Just enough horseradish. The red powdery stuff on top and that airy yellow fluff with a little bite. The cold, wet, chalky shell holding it all together. I started walking toward the church. "You just gonna leave 'em be?" she asked. I looked back at the eggs that were left, wedged between a plate of cookies and what looked like lemon pie.

I stopped. I'd been trying to do better. To be better.

So I turned back. "Maybe someone gets to the end of the table and realizes they forgot to get deviled eggs."

"So you're leaving them there to help people out?"

"Yeah." I wasn't sure what to say. "I'm thoughtful."

"Nice to meet you, Thoughtful. I'm Cassie."

"All right," I said. "I'm Roy."

"I know that. I'm staying at my uncle's old house for a while. Horace Pennick."

"Can't say I know him."

"He was friends with your grandfather."

"That right?" I asked. She nodded. I wasn't sure what to say. "Guess a lot of people were."

"Yeah. He passed away a few years ago."

"Sorry to hear that."

"Thanks." She nodded, licked some deviled egg off her fingertips, then reached for another egg. "You don't remember me, do you?"

I took another look at her. Tried to picture her younger. Shorter. "No. Should I?"

"I was down here some summers. Family reunions at the civic center. You and Danny Jacobs set that tractor on fire that time?"

"Yeah. I guess I remember that."

"A long time ago."

"Guess it was."

"Looks like we both turned out okay."

"Depends on how you look on it, I imagine."

"I mean, I heard you've been in some trouble. You know, people talking."

"Plenty to go around, you know? Everybody makes their own kind." I looked toward the church, but didn't see my grandmother. Didn't see anyone I knew.

"Yeah." She peeled back the foil on a plate of cookies, taking one and handing me another. Chocolate chip. The thin kind, fresh from the oven, folding over like a Salvador Dali clock in your hands. "I know a little something about trouble myself."

I laughed for the first time in a long while. "Yeah? You put a box of Little Debbies at the front of the table?"

She grinned back. "No." She used the tips of her fingers, pushed loose strands of hair behind her right ear, smiled. "Maybe we can talk about our troubles some other time."

"How come you're always in the shit, son?" Sheriff Modisette asked me, jabbing a red bandana at the flaps under his chin.

I said I didn't know. I looked around the clearing, over to the few acres my grandmother had kept after she'd sold off pieces here and there. A little fishing pond down the hill my grandfather used to like, she'd told me.

The sheriff walked around, looked at the body. "You sure that ain't anybody you know? You willing to swear to that, son?"

"I didn't say that. Just said he wasn't a friend of mine."

"Deputy over there said you said you didn't know this here fellow. You saying the deputy was lying to me?"

"No, sir. He asked me if this was a friend of mine. I said he wasn't."

"You trying to be a wiseass? You got any idea how big a stick I got to fuck a wiseass?"

I said I didn't.

"You telling me you do or you do not know this person we found bereft of breath on your property?"

"Looks like Randy Pribble, Sheriff. But this ain't my property."

"No?"

"No, sir. It's my grandmother's. I don't have any property."

He looked at me, snorted. "No. Don't imagine you do."

Another deputy came along, whispered something to the sheriff. He never took his eyes off me, nodded, started to cough up something, then swallowed whatever it was. "You know how this looks, being right here by y'all's property and all."

I said that yeah, I knew how this looked.

Some people in uniforms and windbreakers were setting numbered cards around the ground, taking pictures, making notes. The sheriff and I walked over to his cruiser. He put his hand on my shoulder, and I pulled away.

"Son, maybe you forgot what happened to Dale Thomas down at the bank? Or maybe you think I forgot?"

"No, sir."

"Maybe you think I don't remember what you did to him?"

"No, sir."

"So you'll understand my interest in having this little chat with you vis-à-vis this here dead man on your property."

"Yes, sir. But I did my time for what happened to Mr. Thomas."

"What happened to Mr. Thomas? Shit, son, *you* happened to Mr. Thomas."

I nodded.

"And I don't need to hear none of your 'extenuating circumstances' bullshit, you hear?"

"Yes, sir."

"And here's Mr. Randall J. Pribble Jr., beaten and deceased, on the property of a violent ex-con. Now, what would you do if you were me?"

I kept my wiseass comments to myself. Shrugged.

"Well, I'll tell you what I'm going to do. I'm going to cover this entire goddamn area with dogs. I'm going to read your account of your whereabouts. I'm going to have deputies walk around and interview your neighbors to see if there's five minutes you can't account for."

"Okay."

"Tell me, son. You get out here much? Last week or so? Last month? Maybe you were out here, I don't know, fishing?"

"No, sir."

"You see over there where the Daltons' line starts?" He pointed off, what seemed far away. I turned to look, and he kept talking. "Couple of my deputies caught some Mexicans up there growing a little cash crop not too long ago."

"I'll be on the lookout," I said.

He shook his head, looked down, and dabbed his forehead before looking back up at me. "I don't need you be on the lookout for no goddamn Mexicans."

I waited for him to tell me what he did need. "Okay."

"I need someone to tell me what the hell is going on here."

"I haven't seen anything, Sheriff. I don't come back here."

"See, that's the thing. We're gonna pull us up some boot prints. You understand what I been telling you? We're gonna fly a copter 'round here. You seen the TV? That CSI? You know how soon we can find out if you're lying to me? That's the shit, son. You understand what I'm telling you? Maybe it was Mexicans growing some more of their weed. Maybe Mr. Pribble was out selling Girl Scout cookies and he stumbled upon them. Maybe it wasn't. Maybe someone whose goddamn property this is was out here with a bunch of Mexicans growing some weed. Right now, I don't know. But we'll find out for damn sure. And if it turns out it's pot growing, well, that's one thing. And if it turns out it ain't, well, that's another."

"Okay."

"Don't you 'okay' me, boy. I'm telling you it's one thing these goddamn Mexicans growing their weed . . . "

He stopped, looked around the woods, shook his head again, working up to some sort of speech. Maybe the sort of election-year crap he delivered at Wednesday Chamber of Commerce luncheons. Letting the dress-shirt crowd know that, sure, they'd had some cases of bad people coming into the county, but by and large, they all made mistakes and when they did he was there and he'd appreciate your continued support. Not long ago I'd worked eleven days washing dishes at the Sweet and Sour Cafe, so I'd gotten to hear him once. He'd been the sheriff for two decades now, and you don't change horses in midstream. If you were growing weed or cooking meth, they'd find you, no matter how untouchable you thought you were. Everyone in the building knew he was talking about Didemus Rudd. They'd gotten him for being tied to some gas station robbery, ended up charging him for all the drugs he had on his property. I'd read all about the hearings in the news. I'd been going through the local want ads in the paper from the day I moved here, and I'd come to find out a good bit about who was on the honor roll, how much the Lions Club raised at their yard sale, and how well some old lady was making out with her cancer treatments. And the crap the sheriff served up at the Chamber of Commerce luncheons.

"I better not find out any of you asshole convicts is trying to bring meth into my county. You ever seen what that does to a woman's face? Shit. Bad enough you nutbags run around tending your goddamn marijuana crops. Farmers, my ass. My daddy and granddaddy farmed this land, son, and you know what they farmed? Hell, no, you don't. They farmed goddamn food, son. They fed their families. Goddamn nutrients. You understand what I'm telling you? You sons of bitches with your goddamn marijuana farms, why, hell, that's one thing. But I'll be John goddamn Brown I let you ruin this county my family built. I find out any of you fuckers is setting up some sort of operation in my county, I will cripple every last one of you." The sheriff waited until I looked him in the eye. "You understand, boy? Abso-fucking-lutely cripple you."

I guess I didn't get the same speech he gave the Chamber of Commerce. "Yeah. I don't know of anything like that, Sheriff. Not my crowd."

He thumped his index finger into the center of my chest. "Better not be, son." He turned and walked away.

I got back to my grandmother's house in time for her to reheat me some chicken and dumplings before she went to bed.

"Sheriff find you?" she asked.

"Yes, ma'am."

"Asking about that Pribble boy?"

"Yes, ma'am."

"On our property?"

I nodded, mouth full of dinner, said he was pretty close.

"That can't look too good, Roy. Not good at all." She shook her head. "You tell them you were with me the whole time?"

I nodded.

"Course, they'll just think I'm lying for you. Still, though." She shook her head, looked at the ceiling, then closed her eyes. "Wonder what the Pribble boy was doing wandering around the woods."

I said I wasn't sure.

She took a deep breath, clicked her tongue, letting me know she was changing subjects. "You know, I hear Cassandra Pennick is learning to be a doctor."

"That right?"

"Not the medical doctor, mind. The P-h-D kind."

"Sounds smart."

"And cute, too. Don't you think?"

"Hadn't noticed."

"You noticed her twenty years ago," she said.

"What do you mean?"

"Maybe not twenty. Near about that, I guess. When you and her and Uncle Fed's two boys used to play around here."

"I don't remember that," I said, folding the last dumpling onto the tip of the fork, dragging it along the bottom of the bowl, picking up the leftover specks of cornbread.

"Over where that Mitchell boy put up that trailer."

"All right."

"Might be a good time to go through all them boxes in the back. The girl was asking some questions."

"About us?"

"About everybody. Got Birdie Cassels talking for plumb near three hours, from what I hear. Of course, reckon it seemed a mite longer for the girl than for Birdie."

"What's she talking about?"

"Her doctor work. Country folks, what they're saying. She's staying in her uncle's house for a while. They say she's going around talking about life around here. How it used to be. What's changed. All that sort of thing."

"Sounds like a bad idea, all that looking behind you."

"Why's that?"

"Folks like to ask questions, write stuff down on notepads. Make a list of what you've done. Like you're a sickness needs treating."

"I think the Pennick girl is just interested in the area and her family. What everyone around here has done."

"Everything everybody's done?" I shook my head, took the bowl to the sink. "Not like a history lesson's likely to help anybody." I rinsed the bowl, set it on the dishtowel to dry.

She chuckled, turned a lamp off, headed for bed. "You never know, Roy."

I was trimming around the headstones at the Western Cemetery when a sheriff's deputy waved at me from behind the parsonage, which had been empty for the past year or so. I leaned the weedeater against Jasper Womack's stone and walked through the tall grass to the chainlink fence.

The old black and tan coonhound I'd shared my sandwich with came from behind the Mosley headstones, fell into step with me, nosing my hand as I walked.

The deputy—Skinny Dennis McWilliams—leaned down, pulled a sprig of crabgrass from along the fence, and slid it into his mouth. "Looks like a good dog you got there."

"Stray," I said, scratching the dog behind his floppy ears. "Go on, Buddy. Get."

"Not much of a stray if you named the little guy."

"Gotta call him something. Dog doesn't care."

"Guess that's right. He much help cleaning up around here?"

"Naw," I said. "More trouble than he's worth." Pointed to the shed on the edge of the yard. "Caught him trying to put two-stroke in the mower. Coulda ruined the whole engine."

McWilliams grinned. "That right?"

"Yeah. But he works cheap, so I keep him around."

The deputy made a point of giving the cemetery a long look-over while I waited for him to say what he'd come for. "I always cut the yard first, then come back and weed-whack. You telling me I'm doing it wrong?"

I looked around the cemetery, the weeds around the head-stones cut down into stalks along the ground, the grass growing up in clumps between the rows, mostly down in the low, soggy area where the Talleys were buried.

"Mower won't be fixed til tomorrow," I said. "Getting a little ahead of the game is all. Nobody much cares how you clean up a mess, long as you do."

McWilliams nodded. My dad had coached him in high school when the Waldo Wildcats went undefeated. That had been a long time ago, but he still felt some sort of connection, I guess. He'd gotten me out of some trouble a few months ago when he probably shouldn't have. "Good to get ahead when you can," he said. "Makes things easier." He shifted the weed around in his mouth. "Never know when the next storm's gonna pop up."

I knew what he wanted to talk about. Deputies don't just drop by to talk about grass cutting. "Something I can help you with, Deputy?"

"Guess I was trying to figure out what happened out in the woods the other day." He took the weed from his mouth.

"I already talked to the sheriff."

"You ever see anything out of the ordinary? Shorter plants. You know," he waved around the cemetery, "weeds."

"I'm not really what you'd call an agricultural expert. Sheriff said he'd caught someone out there, I believe."

"Roy, you ever hear the expression 'don't shit where you eat'?"

I nodded.

"You ever hear the same kind of expression about not growing your illegal crop on your own property?"

"That's a weird expression."

McWilliams grinned again. "Maybe it's more like a rule of thumb, then. You been following this Didemus Rudd case?"

"The drug dealer?"

"Alleged."

"What I read in the paper."

He picked up another weed, peeled it apart as he talked. "Why don't you just spray the weeds, you don't mind my asking? Instead of always moving around and cutting them down."

I wiped my sleeve against the sweat dripping into my eyes. "Don't know. Never thought about it much." I turned and looked around at the cemetery. "Lotta dead folks, though. Be a lot of poison to get rid of all the weeds."

"Easier just to cut them down when they crop up?"

"I guess."

"But you have to see them come up. Sometimes they spread out and you can't tell what's a weed. I mean, you think something might be a weed, or maybe it's harmless. Maybe it's grass. Maybe it's crabgrass. Hell, maybe it's an oak tree trying to come up. Then the next thing you know, all these weeds have grown up and they're all of a sudden choking the life out of the decent plants."

"Deputy, I get the feeling you're going the long way around the barn to get to something."

"Roy," he said, then took a breath. "I need your help."

"That right?"

"You know your dad was the first real coach I had, playing ball."

I said I knew that.

"We had a couple good pitchers on the team. Pat Crawford. Andy Daniels. But Andy gets hurt in a game, snaps his elbow, and your dad takes me over off the field and spends a few minutes showing me how to pitch."

"Okay."

"Not throw. Pitch. Takes a while. He sends me out to the mound and I walk the first few guys I see, then give up a grand slam. I think we lost that one by fifteen runs."

"You going to tell me to practice my weed cutting?"

"I'm going to tell you what your dad told me." He flicked away what was left of the weed he'd been chewing. "He said I needed to get off my ass and do something I could be proud of. He said you can't schedule opportunity, Roy. It just shows up when it feels like it."

When I got back to my grandmother's, she and Cassie Pennick were sitting in old, metal lawn chairs, sharing a pitcher of iced tea.

I guess I could have talked to them about what the deputy had been trying to get me to do. Or I could have gone right to my cousin, Cleo. Told him what the deputy wanted. I could have talked to somebody, I guess. Maybe that's what people do when they get their problems. They talk to their wives or their shrinks or their preachers. I could have done that, if I'd had anybody, I guess.

"That deputy find you?" my grandmother asked as I walked up.

"Yes, ma'am."

"Popular fellow these days," she said.

"Guess so."

"He give you any trouble?"

"No, ma'am."

"Give him any?"

"Hardly any."

She nodded to Cassie. "Roy, I think you know Miss Pennick."

"A little," I said.

My grandmother got up, said she had to check something in the kitchen.

Cassie tried to set her glass down quietly on the metal table, but it clanged anyway. For a minute she scraped her fingernail along the outside rim of the table, flecks of rust falling off like snowflakes. "Roy, I said my uncle knew your grandfather."

"Yeah."

"Well, there was a little more to it than that."

✦ ✦ ✦

Ever since Didemus Rudd had gotten arrested, folks had been fighting to be the county's king of pot, Deputy McWilliams had said. The pot king and the meth mob. Pot took lots of land, but meth was a kitchen operation. Rudd and Sawyer could fight over the cash crop, he'd said, while your neighbor was cooking meth all by himself.

I'd always tried my best to steer clear of all that, but it didn't always work out that way.

"Your father was a good man, Roy. He helped me out in a lot of ways. And now there's some shit going on around here I need your help with. Everything's a little mixed up right now. Just getting worse. People aren't thinking about what they're doing. They're just doing. The Sawyers and Pribbles and, between me, you, and the coonhound over there, probably a handful of people wearing badges."

Badges. No badges. Ex-con. All those little boxes they want to put you in. Yeah, my father was a good man. What's that to me? I'm supposed to coach a baseball team? I'm supposed to do what the cop asks me to because he knew my father? I knew enough about cops to know that the first thing they do is look at your history. Not Cassie's kind of history, either.

Driving along the highway, I kept thinking about what Cassie had told me that afternoon after my grandmother had gone inside.

Cassie sat up in her chair, elbows on her knees. "You know my uncle and your grandfather worked together?"

"You said they were friends."

"Work, too."

"At the place up in Bradley?" The last job he'd had before he was killed.

"No. Not that kind of work. They did jobs together, but not like 'a job,' you know."

"All right." The late afternoon sun was pressing down, the sort of heat so heavy that it weighs on the dirt, pushes it so much that it starts to float back up into the air, like some sort of reverse evaporation, getting dust into everything you've got.

"Your grandmother and I started talking a little about it. About how my uncle was always into something. About how that's how come we're all here now." She shifted in the chair. "How come I am, I guess. Come back home, kinda. Not sure if I should have been saying anything. Just . . . " She looked off behind me as a truck rattled along the dirt road, scratching gravel into the ditch. "It's just, some of it is hard to talk about, you know?"

"Yeah. Don't worry about it," I said. "Just tell what you want to tell."

She nodded. "Your grandmother reminded me about when we were kids. She said how we played together a couple of times when I was here. Guess she remembers more than either one of us."

"Yeah. She mentioned it to me."

"Don't really remember it. I mean, I remember some stuff from back then, but, I don't know."

"Like maybe it was a TV show you're remembering?"

"Exactly. Like I'm kinda detached from it."

"Detached," I nodded.

"They oughta bottle that, you know? Detachment."

"I'm pretty sure they do."

She grinned. "Not sure my insurance would cover it."

I tried to think of something to say. Tried to imagine I was someone else for a second, someone who knew what to say. My dad. A preacher. Some counselor saying the right thing.

"I got a college question to ask you," I said. "You ever read a book with a line goes 'we live as we dream—alone'?"

"Sounds familiar," she said. "What's it from?"

"Don't know. Some guy said it to me a while ago." Seemed like a long while ago.

"You know what comes next?"

"With what?"

"The next line. Like is it something about how we dream alone so we have to work together, have to live together? Like that's what draws us together. If we have this shared aloneness, then we have a shared trait."

"That's not the sense I got."

"Okay. Because now that you mention it, that's a big part of my dissertation. How rural life offers a continuity of identity because of the group dynamic."

"If you say so."

"No, see, what I mean is how in an urban area you have people coming and going and they can recreate their identities twenty times a day. In rural America, everyone knows your whole history and your parents' history."

"I guess."

"I suppose that's why I find it, I don't know, reassuring coming back to the area."

"How's that?"

"Like you can fit right in. Horace Pennick's niece. People have some idea what to expect. I'm not just a stranger like I'd be in a big city, say New York or Chicago or Memphis."

I said all right.

"Or that's what I thought, anyway. I came down here, thinking, you know, I'd get into it. The country. The visiting here when I was a kid. My parents being from here. My family. Kind of like a genealogy thing. Like I could connect with people. Get something real. But I just don't know anyone. I'm still on the outside looking in. You know? It's like sometimes I'm all right and don't think about it, and sometimes I'm like that person who comes in and the guy says, 'Today the part of Cassandra Pennick will be played by someone else.'"

"The soap operas?"

"Yeah. Like that. Like the TV show. I don't know. I just had this idea about coming back and fitting in. And now I'm feeling like maybe I didn't even fit in then. I just didn't know it back then."

"Sure."

"But there's this role for me. And I can't find it. People expect something of me and, I don't know." She looked out toward the sun. "Just not like I thought it was coming back here, and I'm not sure what to do, you know?"

"I think that's how everybody feels," I said.

"Yeah?"

"Maybe. Maybe everybody thinks about their roots. Like getting back to them. But then you get back and everything has been cut down."

"And it's not like it was in your mind."

"If you can really remember what it was like."

"I had this list," she said. "Like a family tree. I was asking people what they remembered of people. You could say, 'Tell me what you remember of John Doe,' and one person would say one thing and one another. Like the person only existed in relation to others."

"So that's what you're writing about?"

"I don't know about that anymore." She looked at me, took a breath. "Roy, when I asked them about your grandfather, everyone said the same thing. Said he was a good man. Everybody. I just thought you'd want to know."

"Okay."

"And I don't know, you know, how he died or what happened. But everybody says he was a good man. Just a few people remember, but it's what they all say."

"Your uncle, too," I said. "I'm sure they were both good men."

"He was. Honestly. He really was. He just got caught up in it. I think he thought it was all just little stuff he had to do to keep going. Nothing big. Just little things."

"A buck from the tip jar. A five from the offering plate?"

"Something like that, I suppose."

"How's that?"

"He got tired of all those little things. One time he said something about looking behind you at all the footprints you've left. Like on a trail."

"Yeah?"

"I came down to stay with him after my mom got sick. This was seven years ago. I remember he said that you look ahead, and where the trail should be clear, there's all these footprints laid out for you. Because of what you've already done, all those steps or missteps, you're just going to keep going. He said he finally understood what your grandfather was talking about."

"Talking about what?"

"I don't know. That's what he said. Trying to change paths, I thought. He said he finally understood why your grandfather had done it. Had tried to do it."

"That's what happened to my grandfather?"

"I don't know, Roy. I wish I did. But I think that's what happened to my uncle. The more I'm back here, the more I'm talking to people. He was talking about how your grandfather had decided to take a different trail. It was like he wanted to do what your grandfather had done. I mean, I didn't know your grandfather, and I guess I didn't remember so much about you and your grandmother. It was like he was just talking about people from a book. But now that I'm back here and talking to you and talking to your grandmother, I don't know. It's starting to come together now."

I got to Cleo's mid-afternoon, parked over where he'd hung a sign for his bayou tours. I heard a pop-pop and walked around behind his house. He'd set up what looked like archery targets.

"'Sup, cuz?"

"Teaching those targets a lesson?"

"Shit, yeah. You know Elvis himself used to do it like this. This guy was telling me about it. He's on a tour of the South, this guy. From Chicago. Said he was at Graceland, the whole back of the place is tore up to shit. The King, he'd hang targets on the back wall, stand in the yard, and shoot back at the house. Said it looks like a wasp's nest back there, all full of holes."

"Well, as long as you got something to aim for."

"Got some bananas and peanut butter and shit, gonna make me some fried Elvis burgers here in a bit."

"Ah, just ate," I said. "Got your message. What's going on?"

Cleo put the pistol in his waistband, bumped a cigarette out of a pack. "Let's go inside."

We stood around his kitchen table as he laid out the peanut butter, the honey. Pulled a banana from the top of the fridge, started slicing it.

"Randy Pribble," he said.

"Yeah. Heard about that."

"Smart guy. A fucking prodigy, that guy."

"Maybe he shoulda smartened up a little more," I said.

"Hell, Roy. This shit don't make you smarter. Just makes you older."

I said all right.

"Thing is, he was supposed to do this thing with me. He kinda started to chicken out 'cause of this new girl he was seeing. Getting pussy-whipped and shit, I guess. Figure it doesn't matter now, but I still gotta do this thing."

"What thing?"

"You know Chet Dalton?"

"Ballplayer?"

"No. Hank Dalton's son. The mini-mart store that got robbed a while ago."

"Yeah. Seems vaguely familiar, I guess."

"Guy thinks he's big shit, right? Figure he's been skimming here and there. Randy and I had a couple things lined up, but first we were supposed to go visit with the guy."

"To do what?"

"Shit, have a talk with the guy. Show him the error of his ways. Thou shalt not steal fromest thou employer and shit like that."

"Seems simple."

"Yeah. People get to complicating this shit, that's when you're fucked, man. Gotta play it smart."

"Simple and smart. Got it."

"You want to hear something smart? So Randy and that Crawford guy from the grocery store, we were doing this job about a month ago. So the Crawford guy goes into the house, unplugs the fridge, turns off the AC, opens all the windows."

"What for?"

"That's what I said. Turns out, they make the house dead quiet so they can hear if someone drives up."

"No shit?"

"Yeah. Then it's like everything slows down and you get your shit done, know what I'm saying? It's like everything stops for you." Cleo tapped the table in broken rhythm. "Maybe this shit does make you smarter."

We parked my truck along the road in front of the house with no front yard, got out, walked to the house.

Cleo asked if I was ready. I nodded, felt the heaviness of the shotgun I was carrying.

I walked around back of the house, waited on the steps of planks and milk crates. When I heard the front door open, I walked in through the back. Through the kitchen of brown jars and rags and a trash can towered with paper plates. I set the unloaded shotgun on the kitchen counter, walked into the front room, a mess of potato chip bags and CD cases where rugs should have been. "Sorry to interrupt your afternoon nap," Cleo said as Chet stood up from the couch. "We just wanted to have a visit. A mutual friend asked us to stop by."

Chet worked his tongue around his bottom teeth, looked at Cleo, then back at me. Maybe he was seeing if we were armed. Maybe he was seeing where the closest door was. Maybe he was planning how to get to wherever his gun was.

He asked us what the fuck we thought we were doing, coming into his house. Said we'd just made a big fucking mistake.

"Chet Dalton?" Cleo asked, turning back to me. "This is Chet Dalton, right? We got the right address from Sawyer, right?"

"Shit," Chet said. "Sawyer?"

"Yeah. 'Shit' is right, pal. Which is what you're in right now."

Cleo hiked his chin at me, and I pulled the shotgun with me into the room. Racked a shell into the chamber.

Cleo turned back to Chet. "Here's what going to happen. I'm going to ask you a couple of questions. They'll be easy fucking questions. You don't do anything but answer those questions. You don't say shit, all right? That clear?"

Chet said it was.

"Nice TV," Cleo said, nodding at the big screen against the wall.

"Just got it yesterday."

Cleo lifted his arm, blasted a shot into the screen. "That wasn't a question I asked, motherfucker."

Chet said "Jesus" and sat down into the couch.

I sat down on a desk against the wall, the shotgun in my lap.

"You know the payday loan place up on 82?" Cleo said to me the next day.

"Couple of them."

"The blue and gold one. By the old grocery store." Cleo pulled a knife from his kitchen drawer, reached into his fridge, and came out with some cheese.

"Yeah."

"They cash in and outta there all the time. Randy and me been watching the place. Couple days, it's like the planets lining up. Government checks hit in the morning. And their weekly delivery from their corporate office gets there in the afternoon. The money that went out comes back in. The money going out ain't left yet. Only happens every so often like that. Pull this off, got one more lined up next week, maybe lie low for a couple weeks after that."

"Sounds like you got it figured out."

"Yeah. Randy had it all worked out. Until he up and got himself killed."

"Any idea what happened with that?"

"No." He looked away, shook his head. "None. My guess is he was playing both sides of the fence, you know? Kinda squirrelly like that."

"Guess I didn't know him that well."

"Weren't missing much. But he woulda loved to shoot that Dalton boy's TV."

"Guy seemed pretty attached to his TV," I said.

"Probably pissed he won't get to watch Oprah. You see him start to cry?" Cleo bit a piece of sliced cheese from his knife. "Anyway, Randy and me was going to do this payday loan thing. Was figuring, seeing how the Dalton thing worked out, maybe you and me might do this one, too. Two-man job."

"You got a plan?"

"Step one: Walk in with guns. Step two: Walk out with the cash."

I said that sounded easy enough. Then I asked about the job the other day, where they'd unplugged the refrigerator, turned off the air-conditioning. "Where was that?"

"Old lady Dawson. Lives out past that Methodist church that burned down."

"Dawson? Ettie May Dawson?"

"I don't know. Sounds right. Why?"

I wanted to tell him she's a friend of my grandmother's. That she was fighting cancer. Pancreatic. I wanted to tell him I'd seen her not two weeks ago with my grandmother and they were both talking about how expensive coffee had gotten. How she was saying her grandson didn't like to come over to her house because she didn't have any video games to play. "That's out by my grandmother's," I said.

"No shit? You wanted us to stop by and say 'hello'?"

"She's a friend of my grandmother."

"Oh. Well, fuck me, Roy. Just say so. Just give me a list of people who are off-limits, then." He laughed, shook his head. "Shit, man. You serious? Jesus, Roy."

"I don't know. Just getting a little too close."

"Yeah. Ain't everything? Hell, Roy, you gotta know by now you got something people want then people gonna take it away at some point. Woman had two rings in her underwear drawer must be worth something nice. Planning to head over to Texarkana this weekend and see, you wanna come?"

"That's all right."

"What the hell's eating you?"

"Nothing," I said.

"Hell, you been sounding like a pussy last week or two. Something got into you? I mean, shit, the Dalton thing was pretty easy, you know. But this payday thing. Fuck, man. You gotta be on your game. Fuckers take this shit serious."

"Naw," I said. "Just thinking about what it is we're doing, you know?" I pulled a sleeve of crackers from a box, popped two at a time into my mouth.

Cleo pointed the knife at me. "That's your goddamn problem, right there. You don't think, man. You just do the thing."

I rolled my eyes, said yeah, fine.

"I ain't shitting you, Roy. You get to a point in your life, it's called growing up. You don't think about what you're doing. You just do it. Some shit you gotta do ain't easy, right? It's the adult shit."

I said I guessed he was right.

"You don't have to believe in what you're doing, man. You don't gotta build up a big church to it or fuck it and shit. You just have to do it. Hell, you can think about it later. You just do the shit you gotta do. That's what being a fucking grownup is all about."

+ + +

"I don't know, Roy," McWilliams said. "Not like we can just call up those records. They're not digitized."

"So how would you find out?"

"We'd request the files. Send it through the department. Somebody might want to know why all the interest in your grandfather all of a sudden."

"Not all of a sudden." I set the air hose to the side, shut off the compressor. The sun was right overhead, putting you right in the middle of your shadow, the gravestones an occasional sparkle of granite.

Deputy McWilliams was standing in the doorway. He leaned into the shed a little more, squinted. "Well, that's how it might look, you know. How much equipment you got in here? Someone must have spent a small fortune at one time."

I walked to the building, looked around at the walls, the shelves. A couple push mowers, weed whacker, wheelbarrow with a tire I needed to plug. Chainsaw. Axe. This and that. "Whatever they spent, it was a long time ago."

"Guess you're right. You keep all this running?"

"Yeah." I shut the door, snapped the padlock.

"Didn't know you were a mechanic."

"Not really."

"Takes something to handle all this. Engines and all. Must be good with your hands."

I shrugged. "Just do what's gotta be done."

"Right. Roy, speaking of that, you wanted to see me about something."

"I did." I wiped a layer of oil off my palm, slid the rag into my back pocket. "You talk to Randy Pribble lately?"

"Kind of a one-sided conversation, I'd imagine."

"Before he died, I mean."

"Now, Roy, that's an odd question to be asking." He stretched his arms, let his right hand rest on his holster. "What would cause you to ask a question like that?"

I wasn't sure exactly why I was asking, but I was starting to regret locking the door to the axe. "I heard Randy was what you might call a double agent."

"Well, it's possible from time to time he had information that might be useful in an investigation, if that's what you're asking."

It wasn't. "Snitch?"

"Some people help when they can. You know, see the error of their ways. And some get locked up. Something you're getting at?"

"Just thought maybe somebody found out, maybe something happened."

"You got a somebody in mind?"

I said I didn't. Said it wasn't much my concern.

The deputy agreed with that much. "That what you wanted? Tell me about the Pribble boy? Something you'd heard from your cousin?"

I'd been thinking about what Cassie said, how her uncle had been looking at a different path. How maybe that's what my grandfather had done.

The path Cassie had talked about, each choice is a step. I wasn't so sure about that. In Haven House each choice was a pebble. Each choice is a lot of mumbo jumbo for the self-help crowd at church. The problem is you don't really know which choice is going to help, which one is going to get you in deeper. I could do fifty different things at the moment, and there'd be no telling which one was the right one.

"Something like that," I said, giving as much thought as I could to what my grandfather would have done. Another job with Cleo. Then another, until we ended up at some old lady's house, taking her wedding ring from her drawer.

Or push it to a point and decide you're not going any further. Find a new trail, like Horace Pennick had said. Maybe that's what happened to my grandfather on the road from Bradley. Or maybe I could figure out what my dad would have done. Doing the straight thing all along, by the rules. Rotary Club. Coach baseball. But it was too late for that. At some point, it doesn't matter what you do. You get far enough down one trail, doesn't matter much which way you go from there—they're all the wrong choices. Some days you just do what you learned to do, what you've lived your life doing. A body tumbling down a hill, into a ravine.

When you're on your own, standing in front of a deputy in the middle of a cemetery, I guess it doesn't matter as much. When everyone knows what you've done, what kind of person you are. You're in the dark, with no one around. At Haven House, they'd say they can tell if you're a good person by what you'd do at a stoplight at three in the morning, no one around. Do you follow the rules when no one is looking? I asked the lady why was I out at three in the morning, all alone. She said it didn't matter. But it does. How you got into the middle of the darkness is what matters the most, I told her. Why you were alone. She wrote down that I refused to answer.

You get to that point, that stoplight. Maybe whether you stop or go isn't what's important. Maybe what's important is that you move at all, that you keep moving in one direction until morning. Because you have somewhere to go. And maybe she was right. Maybe it doesn't matter why you were out at three in the morning. Maybe what matters is where you are a few hours later. Maybe that's what makes you better. Not what you were doing in the middle of the night in Bradley. What matters is that you were on your way home.

Hell, maybe that's what happened to Randy Pribble, but then he stopped to turn around. And now the deputy was down one snitch.

"I think I got something might help you, Deputy."

"So the deputy wasn't much help with your grandfather?" Cassie asked the next morning. My grandmother had found some excuse for Cassie to come over for a late breakfast, then found another excuse to leave.

"Said wasn't a lot he could do." I leaned back in the rocking chair while Cassie eased back and forth in hers. I set my coffee down on the table between us, pressed my feet against the boards until I was nearly leaning against the house.

"Did he say whether the case was still open?"

"No. Don't know it matters much whether it's open. Not what you might call high on their to-do list."

"Guess they're still looking at the Pribble murder." Cassie blew the heat off her coffee, took quick, narrow sips.

"I imagine so."

Somewhere through the woods cows were mooing back and forth. "Sure is nice around here," Cassie said a while later.

"Used to be you could sit on the porch early mornings and listen to cows and frogs hollering at each other till lunch," I said.

"Peaceful."

"Yeah. And that gritty rattle of wheels on the gravel road out there and maybe a shot or two, somebody gets a deer."

Cassie closed her eyes. "'Gritty rattle.' I like that."

"Well, that was a long time ago. All you get now is chainsaws and woods all stripped to hell."

"At least it's pleasant."

"Unless you're a tree," I said.

"Or a Pribble."

"Guess so."

She took a deep breath, seemed to look out past the tree line. "Must have been something when my uncle and your grandpa were running around out here."

I rocked forward in my chair, walked to the edge of the porch. "Yeah. Long time ago."

"Sure seems like the stakes were lower, you know?"

"Guess I don't."

"I mean the bad stuff wasn't all that bad."

"Still not sure what you're getting at."

"My uncle. He told me the big goings-on here back in the day. Stills. Running numbers. Cockfights."

"He said that's what he did?"

"Yeah. And he was trying to get out of it."

"Yeah."

"You think they were running numbers? Uncle Horace and your grandpa."

"I don't think so."

"You know what 'running numbers' means?"

"Yeah," I said.

"You sure?"

"No."

She grinned. "I didn't, either, until my uncle decided he finally wanted to talk about it. For my dissertation. The impact of cultural isolation on economic development in rural America."

"That right?"

"It means—"

"Means why are country folks so poor," I said. "I got that. Just wasn't sure what numbers running was is all. Some kind of gambling."

"It's like the lottery, back before the state had a lottery. Everyone in the community picks numbers, puts in their money. Lot of places, especially rural and dense urban areas, still run numbers, mainly because of their distrust of the government."

"Sounds about right."

"Sounds so quaint, doesn't it?" She stood up, walked up next to me. "Like it's little men in fedoras and suspenders writing out numbers on a chalkboard. Taking money around to people. All the money wrapped up in brown paper like it's some kind of fish."

"I wouldn't think it was like that," I said.

"Right. I'm sure it wasn't. I'm sure there were guns and knives and bodies. The night I left Little Rock to come down here, you know what the top three stories on the news were?"

I said I didn't.

"Homicides. Unsolved homicides. Three in a row. I thought it would be different here. I mean, coming back to the country. Back in time. A simpler place."

"Yeah."

"I mean, I know it wasn't always idyllic, of course. I know there's still crime. But, still. Don't you ever get tired of it, Roy? Of all the violence? Of everybody pulling a gun on everybody?"

I said that, yeah, I get tired of a lot of things.

"If Uncle Horace was just running numbers, I mean." She shook her head, looked away. "I don't know what I mean. And he was trying to get out. I guess I've just been overthinking it all."

"Lot of that going around."

"Not enough, seems like," she said. "You see that bird on the fence post there? Haven't seen one in years. Red-winged blackbird. Used to see them all the time. Now, in the city, I don't ever see them. And down here, they're all over. Same birds. Same fields. Like fifty years ago. A hundred."

I took a step closer to her, looked out where she was facing, tried to see what she saw.

✦ ✦ ✦

"So, Cassandra Pennick doing okay?" my grandmother asked as I was helping her put away groceries.

I told her Cassie was okay, asked her about my grandfather, his jobs.

"This and that," she said. "Whatever needed doing."

I asked her what he was doing the week he was killed.

"Up in Bradley, fixing engines," she said. "Back then there was a lot more call for that." She took a long sip of her sweet tea, spun the glass between her hands. "Lot more call for everything."

I said that yeah, there was.

"Roy, you gotta remember, back then people didn't leave the county for much, 'cept for they want to get a little out-of-state liquor over at Ray's. But that's about as far into Union County as most people went. Maybe some folks had kin over in Lafayette. Folks stayed close to home. Now you got people driving two hours to work in an office building so they can eat their lunch at their desk. I was talking to Birdie Cassels of a morning and she said her son Luke, the one with the glass eye, drives clear to Monroe for work. Not even in the same state. I asked her what he did, and she said she didn't know. Didn't know what her own son does for a living. Said her boy Mark works for a septic company outside Camden, and Matt sells those modular homes up in Magnolia. But she didn't have any idea how to explain to me what Luke does for a living. Something with banking, she said. Everybody's driving off in their cars and moving away and eating lunches at their desks, she said. Said Luke's new wife doesn't even know how to cook. He stops at the Texaco on the way to work to get a sandwich. At least that girl of hers stayed close to home." She shook her head. "Bad enough your granddaddy had to go to Bradley, but at least I knew what he was doing there."

"Fixing engines?"

"That's right."

I handed her the picture I'd had in my pocket. "Him on the left?"

"That's your granddaddy," she said. "And Horace Pennick there on the right."

"And the man in the middle?"

She adjusted her glasses, pulled the picture closer. "Reckon I knew him some time. Can't rightly say who it is now, though. Where'd you find this picture? I don't think I've ever seen this."

"In the back, in some of the boxes of Mom and Dad's stuff. I was looking for—I don't know what I was looking for."

"Well, you found this picture of whoever it is."

"Yes, ma'am. Think they might have worked together?"

"What you want to know that for, Roy?"

"I just was figuring, you know, who he might have worked with. Who they were, I guess."

"I know Mr. Pennick and your granddaddy worked for a while, but I can't say I remember that fella."

"Think Mr. Jenkins might know?"

"Jenkins?"

"The old man past Mr. Tatum's house. Used to be in those TV shows. Got me the job cutting grass at the church."

"Spencer Jenkins? Heck, boy, he's not any older than I am."

"Think he might know?"

"I stopped trying to figure out what people know and what they don't a long time ago. Got to where I wanted to know, I just asked them."

I parked my truck behind the Qwik-Mart, walked through a couple empty lots to meet Cleo by the payday loan place.

He asked if I was ready. I put the gloves on, said I was. He led me to the alley beside the place, kneeled against the blue brick wall, then rolled a shotgun out of a blanket and handed it to me. I pulled down the ski mask as he went over the plan again.

A couple cars went by, but no one noticed us. No one ever did.

I knew my grandfather didn't spend all his time in Bradley working on engines. He'd been involved in jobs with Horace Pennick. That much was certain. But there wasn't any record of either one of them ever getting arrested. Not that I could find, anyway. Maybe they were better at it than I was. Than Cleo was. Still, Cleo and I were alive and they weren't.

I checked the shotgun, and he handed me some extra shells. "Thought we weren't going loaded for bear."

"Nah," Cleo said. "Shit starts to break nasty, you gotta be prepared."

I pulled out one of the shells. "Birdshot?"

"Yeah. So don't worry. For show, right?"

I said fine, put the shell back.

"Besides, they don't want to get shot. They got families. Mortgages. Shit like that. Like we said. Go in. Get the money. Go home." Cleo pulled down his mask and edged to the front corner of the building.

I found the back door unlocked, just as Cleo had said. Saw the cigarette butts in a dirt pile by a lawn chair, the smokers' stone for propping the door open.

I put my hand on the door handle, flexed my glove. The day before I could have done fifty different things, taken fifty different paths. I could have followed the trail back out of the woods and found a whole new path. One that hadn't already been blazed with a path for me. One that hadn't been chopped to pulp. The day before, I could have done so many things.

I took a breath, walked into the back of the building, and eased shut the door behind me.

PART TWO

Skinny Dennis McWilliams pulled a frozen Tupperware bowl from his freezer, slid it into the microwave, and sat down at the table, raking tablecloth crumbs onto the floor.

He picked up the message, looping ink on a sheet of cross-shaped notepaper. At the top of the cross, sideways to fit, Cora had written, "Dinner in freezer. 5 minutes on medium." Then, on the cross part, "2 minutes on high. Don't forget Bandit." And underneath, sideways again, "half can in the morning, dry all day, quarter at night. Call when I can. Be EXTRA careful. Smooch."

Another mission trip. At least he wouldn't have to box up any more Bibles or shoes.

He set his head down on the table, fell asleep for the half minute until the oven beeped. Five minutes on high.

He dropped the bowl on the table, pulled the dripping lid off, tossed it near the sink. Took a spoon from the drain board, stirred the chili. Beans like pebbles, meat like mud. He lowered the bowl to the floor, called the dog. Then he took a longneck from the fridge and watched a half inning of the Astros until Caskey called.

"Game time," Caskey said, opening the passenger door.

"Game time?"

"It's my new battle cry."

"Got your game face on?" McWilliams grinned, sliding into the seat, working the seatbelt buckle around his holstered pistol.

"Oh, shut up. Just trying to get in the mood to do some damage. So we all set?"

"Pretty much. I'll go in, need you to hang back."

"Why's that?"

"Need to keep it low-key."

"This the Alison guy's idea?"

"No," McWilliams lied. "We just don't want some Butch and Sundance standoff. Keep it low. Manageable."

"You go in, and I'll hang back?"

"Yeah."

"I'm thinking it's better we both go in front, if there's two of them in there armed."

"There's only Porterfield you have to worry about."

"You sure?"

"Yeah. Roy said he's a loose cannon, liable to snap we come in there like some overpowering threat."

"I think overpowering threat is the way to go."

McWilliams nodded, took a breath. "Remember that bank guy, Dale Thomas?"

"One your guy and Porterfield beat the shit out of? Yeah. I remember."

"Seems Porterfield's the one went ballistic on the guy."

"That what happened?"

"Yeah. Roy and his cousin go over there to talk to him about a loan to Roy's grandmother, Dale gets a little mouthy, sends Porterfield off."

"That's what the Alison guy's claiming, huh? He's just a victim of circumstance? Peer pressure? Just trying to get that girl in his eighth grade homeroom to notice? He didn't mean for anyone to get hurt when he beat the shit out of that guy?"

"Sure, fine. Maybe that's not exactly what happened. I don't know. But I figure having you outside as backup is the safer bet. You got the front. There's Roy at the back door. Porterfield in the middle."

"You trust this guy? Roy Alison?"

"I don't trust anybody," McWilliams said.

Caskey shook his head. "We both know that's not true."

McWilliams nodded, watched the houses move to the edge of the windshield as they drove along. "Trust him enough. His father was a good man."

+ + +

McWilliams was sitting at the window of Ned's BBQ when he saw Cleo Porterfield park near the payday loan store across the street, step out with a blanket, and walk into the alley.

"Sweet or un?"

He looked up, saw the waitress with a pitcher in each hand. "Sweet."

She poured his tea, went to the next diners a few booths over.

He'd lost sight of Cleo, but had a good idea what to expect. After three minutes, he stood up as he watched Cleo walk to the front door of the payday loan store.

McWilliams got to his feet, waited for the waitress. "Tell your folks 'hey,'" he said. He left some cash on the table, put on his hat, and walked across the street. He waited behind a white van as Cleo eased into the store and locked the door behind him.

The deputy leaned low around the back of the van, pulled out his radio and called in the armed robbery, then moved to the building, crouching against the brick half-wall under the window.

He'd passed up the chance to warn the people inside, to let them know what he knew. He could have told them they'd gotten a tip about an armed robbery, but he knew what would happen. Everyone would talk about it. No one would show for work. And nothing would happen. Everyone would be protected for that moment. For that fifteen minutes. But not the moments that followed. Not the next day when some drug dealer would sell a bag of weed to a twelve-year-old. Or the next week when someone would be stabbed outside a gas station.

Which is what he'd talked to Roy Alison about at the cemetery.

"Shouldn't we warn the folks?" Roy had asked. "Maybe tell them it's a drill?"

McWilliams had shaken his head, looked out past the gravestones, beyond where his little sister was buried. "You know how many people are out there in the county? People with no idea what's going on? People who just stumble into a bad situation? People killed because of that? Good people? People with their whole lives in front of them?"

Roy hadn't said anything.

"Then there's people out there who want to take all that away. The Rudds and Pribbles and Sawyers. Hell, I got a kid locked up right now who has a good job at the Piggly Wiggly. Got him locked up on conspiracy and home invasion. Know why? I talked to the boy for two hours, and you know what he said? He said he was bored. Bored. You know what happens when those people get bored, Roy? Staci McMahen happens. Every minute those people walk free is another minute you can't let your kid stay out past dark."

"Okay."

"These people, they're not like you and me. They're cold, Roy. They prey on people. They want you to be soft on them, want you to do the right thing. They game the system. So they can just keep doing what they do. They know we have to play by the rules. Because it's what we do. It's what makes us different from them. We're the good guys. We stop the outlaws."

"But can't you let the people at the store know about what's gonna happen? Say it's a drill?"

"Roy, we tell them that, no telling what's likely to happen. We can't have this *not* take place. We have to let this thing work itself out. A robbery like this, we can get you some federal protection. Set it all up. Get the funding like we talked about. But there's got to be a crime. I can't just go handing out money to any people I want to. And besides, we let this look like a fake robbery, there's just no telling what happens. We need it to go down like it's set to go down. Bust you and your cousin.

"We let this one get away from us, we'll never put a stop to this. This is our best shot. And we have to get the two of you in the middle of this. That's the only way this works out for everyone. Otherwise, just no telling."

And he'd meant that. At the time. Then he sneaked a look into the payday loan store and wished he'd warned the people inside. Wished it had just been the man and the woman working behind the counter, without the young couple sitting on the side bench, the husband holding his paycheck stub folded tight in his fist.

When he'd talked to Roy at the cemetery, he'd followed the script. Let the other person think you're on the same team. Talk about the "we" of the situation. Connect. Show him how there's no other way. He'd been through enough training sessions to know what to do, but that didn't mean much in the real situation. He knew he had to convince the informant he had no real choice. You give us the information or you go to prison. For the people who turned out to be informants, there wasn't much choice.

When McWilliams had worked with Randy Pribble, things had been clear. He'd busted the kid a couple of times, but by the third, the kid knew he was in trouble. Convince that kid that his drug-dealing boss doesn't care about him, you're halfway there. Convince him that you do, you're home. Which is what McWilliams had done. What he was good at. Understanding people. Knowing what made them work. When they were in a hole 0-2, standing at the plate, would they take a whack at whatever you threw at them? Would they choke up, foul off pitches until they got what they liked? Would they know you were going to throw the next one in the dirt, just to test them? What would they do with that next chance?

Maybe the Pribble boy went down swinging. Maybe he'd been lucky, living on borrowed time, fouling off pitches. Or maybe Sawyer found out he was working with McWilliams. Maybe the Rudds tracked him down. All McWilliams could do then was tell the paper it was a drug deal gone bad, let the public be on the lookout. Maybe they turn up something. Maybe something shakes out and the sheriff's department gets a lead on something else. Then a week later, just pick out a Mexican the Feds caught in Little Rock or Oklahoma City. Some guy getting deported. Hang it on him. *Based on a lead from a local sheriff's deputy, authorities apprehended the killer at a truck stop in Lawton.* Everyone can go back to tucking their kids in at night. All protected.

Except McWilliams was down one informant, just when he needed him most. Ever since McWilliams had talked to his brother-in-law about the robbery at Hank's place, he'd kept an eye on Cleo Porterfield. Sawyer moving against Rudd meant they were looking at the bottom of the ninth when anything could happen. He needed to have Porterfield and Roy on his team. He knew Porterfield would be an asset because of his involvement in so much small-time work, but Roy Alison would be a great addition, too. McWilliams knew about Roy's past, figured he could look at this as a new chance. A new life. He'd get all the information he could out of Porterfield, then turn him over to the prosecutor. He'd be gone for a long time. But Roy. That was different. He could put Roy back into the situation, maybe he'd fill the void left by Porterfield. Or the Pribble boy.

And in the process he'd be helping the son of his old ball coach. Helping him become a better man. He kept telling himself that. What he had to do was convince Roy. Once he had him on this robbery, he'd have the leverage he needed. Show him there's no choice. Your father was a good man, he'd keep telling him. This is your chance. You can't get away from your family, he'd told Roy at the cemetery. He figured Roy wouldn't feel right about setting up himself and Porterfield. Handing them both over to the cops. But he'd told Roy, sometimes you just have to do this one thing even if you don't believe in it at the time. You just do it and ask forgiveness later.

"I'll let you know," Roy had said. "Anything else?"

"No," the deputy had told him. Then McWilliams had walked across the field, put a flower on his sister's grave. Said a prayer, drove back.

+ + +

McWilliams heard a thin scream from inside, then people shuffling. He looked at the van parked on the street, trying to use the reflection in the windows to see inside. He saw the top edge of the building, power lines, drifting clouds.

He waited to hear Roy sneak to the front, unlock the door. His radio snapped on. Two units were five minutes away. He heard the door lock click.

He drew his pistol, counted to ten. He looked up to see the waitress from across the street walking down the sidewalk, looking back at the payday loan store. Saw her trying to get a view of what was going on. He waved her off, waved to her to get back inside, knew he didn't have much time.

He eased to the door, stood up as he went through, raised his pistol.

"Drop the gun. Hands where I can see them," he said. He held his aim on Cleo Porterfield, standing behind the counter with the woman in charge, gun barrel in her side. In the back of the store, Roy had a man seated at a desk, shotgun at the back of his head.

McWilliams looked around the room, saw the young couple face-down on this side of the counter.

McWilliams said to let the people leave.

Porterfield said to go fuck yourself.

McWilliams took a step to Porterfield, made sure he got a good look at the pistol. "You two, on the ground, stay down and crawl out the door."

As they started to move, Porterfield jabbed his pistol into the woman's side. She made a sound, something like a grunt, and the couple stopped moving.

"I didn't say to stop," McWilliams said, and they started moving again.

"You want a hole in this bitch?" Porterfield asked.

McWilliams knew what he was dealing with, had spent time looking at the man's priors. Robberies, not home invasions. Assaults, not murders. McWilliams would have laid you good odds that Cleo Porterfield had never shot anyone. Ever. "That what you want?"

The couple had reached the door, opened it. McWilliams took another step to the counter, held his gun at Porterfield. He sneaked a peek at Roy standing with the other man, a garbage bag of cash on the desk.

The couple made it through the door. McWilliams heard arms and legs catching as the door closed on them, pressed open again.

In less than two minutes the street would be spotted with cruisers. Sirens and tire squeals, the swish of Kevlar, scuffle of boots. But for this moment, these next two minutes, McWilliams knew he was in control. Two civilians, Roy Alison, himself. And then Cleo Porterfield. McWilliams counted that as four against one.

"Where you think you're going?" Porterfield asked as McWillams came around the counter, pistol held at Porterfield. "Partner, you gonna do something?" he said to Roy.

Roy pumped the shotgun, leveled it back to the man's head.

McWilliams stopped a few feet from Porterfield, both of them even with the counter, the woman between them. McWilliams scanned the area, eyes darting from point to point. Family photos on desk. Corporate calendars. Employee of the month certificates on the walls. "Listen, you want the money. I get that. But Mrs. Martin there doesn't need to be in the middle of this. Just let her go. Let her go home to her two babies. They're counting on her. You don't want the paper to read 'Janice Martin, mother of two, killed in botched robbery' do you?"

"Fuck do I care?" Porterfield spit.

Maybe McWilliams was wrong about him. Maybe he just hadn't had the chance to be the worst person he could be. Then McWilliams saw Porterfield steal a glance at the nearby desk, the photograph of the kids.

Might have a minute left, McWilliams thought. He backed toward Roy, kept his eyes on Porterfield, but moved his aim to Roy's side.

"The fuck?" Porterfield asked.

"Mrs. Martin, I'm sure everything was confusing for you, but do you remember when the deputy and perpetrator struggled? When one of the masked men went for the deputy's pistol and it went off?"

She tried to speak, but the words caught in her throat and she wiped her nose. Porterfield wrapped his arm around her neck, raised the pistol to McWilliams. "Now, let's just all calm the fuck down. You ain't shooting nobody. Leave him the fuck alone."

McWilliams heard a ping, a tiny crack of sound. Then a blast, a small sun exploding in the distance.

Then his head was filled with a list.

A shot. The window. Porterfied down.

A shot. Hot. Fire. On fire.

McWilliams heard the thudding clang of metal on concrete, saw he'd dropped his gun.

The Martin woman screaming toward the front door. The man with Roy falling under the desk.

The fire on his shoulder. Fucking Porterfield got off a shot. Fuck. He reached up with his left hand, pressed the fire on his shoulder, the sticky dampness. Then he knelt to the floor, reached for his pistol.

Movement to his side. He saw Lacewell step into the hall, looking at him. Then he saw Roy with the shotgun, slamming it across Lacewell's arms, the butt of the weapon into his jaw. Roy stepping over him to the back door, garbage bag in hand.

✦ ✦ ✦

"So another couple days?"

"Yeah," McWilliams said to his wife as another little leaguer struck out. "I clear the physical, I can go back the next day." McWilliams used his plastic spoon to dig around the bag of chips. "I think I got ripped off on my Frito pie."

Cora reached across, took the bag out of his slinged arm, the fork. Worked the chips and meat around. "Just have to work at it a little. Get the good parts to the top."

McWilliams said it still looked like mostly chips.

"If they filled it up with meat, how would they make any money?"

"If I wanted a bag of chips, I'd have gotten a bag of chips."

"My, aren't you in a bad mood today?"

He grinned. "Just ready to get back to work. Lotta things to catch up on."

"It's been nice having you around for a couple of days. Much safer, too."

"I wouldn't worry about that. I'll be riding the desk for a while, I imagine."

"You're lucky Owen got there in time, from what the paper says."

"Right. Deputy Owen Caskey. Regular Annie Oakley."

"Good shot, that's for sure."

"Hit his target. Timing left a little to be desired."

"Well, all that matters now is that you're safe." She patted his knee. "They ever catch the other boy?"

"No."

"Y'all find out who it is? That a state secret?"

"No telling," he said. "The guy was a mystery."

"All right," she said, raising her hand over her eyes, looking at the game. "Pitcher for the Tigers seems to be doing a good job. Who is that?"

"That's Champion Tatum's boy."

"This his first game?"

"Yeah."

"Well, he's going to strike out the side again," she said. "Good for him. Not afraid of anything."

"He'll be fine, Cora. Look at him. He's a fighter."

McWilliams watched a boy he didn't know step to the plate, turn up a foot, let the bat fall onto the bottoms of his cleats, clay clumped to the ground. The boy dug in to the batter's box, getting comfortable.

"Planning to stop by Ruby and Hank's this evening to take them some supper. You know Ruby's laid up again."

"Hank Dalton?"

"Yes. You want to come with me?"

"Sure."

Across the back corner of the outfield, in the parking lot, a teenager was talking to a girl. McWilliams watched the girl move to walk away, saw the guy put an arm against the side of the truck, stop her.

The deputy stood up, stretched, felt his holster shift under his arm. He kept his eyes on the parking lot. "Need anything?" he asked Cora. "Getting a hot dog."

"No, I'm fine," she said as she watched her husband walk away.

PART THREE

The day was closing down, and I could hear crickets and frogs in the woods as I made the turn onto Pennick Lane, near the Walkerville Cemetery. I parked in front of the house, where the gravel faded away, and Cassie stepped out onto the porch, left the door open.

She was wearing a bright yellow tank top and cutoff shorts. "Make up your mind yet?"

I stepped out of the truck, leaned against the hood. "About what?"

"About whether you want company."

I looked around for something to do with my hands. "Kind of a one-man deal, I figure."

"Won't matter, then. I'm a woman."

I nodded. Kept it to myself. "Not sure when I'm coming back."

She smiled. "I don't care about that."

"All right."

She set her bag in the bed of my truck, and I closed the door behind her.

"You and that deputy take care of whatever you were working on?" she asked. "All square?"

"Yeah. You eat yet?"

"No," she said. "Thought you might take a girl to dinner."

"Andy's or Dairy Queen?"

"Well, you do know how to treat a girl right, don't you, Mr. Alison?"

"Sky's the limit. As long as we stay under ten bucks."

"So we're going to Magnolia?"

"Athens," I said. "Take care of some business, like I said. We can grab dinner on the way."

"Athens? Georgia or Greece?"

"Arkansas."

"There's an Athens, Arkansas?"

"Kinda near Mena. Didn't you say you lived there for a while?"

"Yeah. Never heard of it."

"It's on the map."

"What's in Athens?"

I leaned forward, pulled the picture from my back pocket, handed it to Cassie. She opened the glove box, held the picture near the light.

"That's my uncle on the right. Who are the other two?"

"My grandpa on the left."

"And in the middle?"

"Franklin Rudd."

"Kin to the folks around here."

"Yeah."

"And he's in Athens?"

"Was this morning."

"And we're going to see him?"

"To talk to him, yeah."

She turned the picture over, looked at the meaningless pencil scrawl on the back, washed out over the years. "You know your grandma's worried about you."

"What makes you say that?"

"She said so."

"Told you that?"

"Yeah, last night. She called."

"I had to go out," I said.

"Said we needed to keep an eye on you. Her and me. Said it seemed like something was going on."

"Yeah."

She set the picture between us, closed the glove box. "That thing loaded?"

"What?"

"The pistol in the glove."

"No."

"You sure you're supposed to have a gun?"

"It's not mine," I said. "Borrowed it off a logger I ran into."

"What's it for?"

"In case Mr. Rudd doesn't want to talk."

"About?"

"What?"

"What might Mr. Rudd not want to talk about?"

"About why he killed my grandpa."

We got to Magnolia and I stopped at the EZ Mart, climbed out to put gas in the truck.

I was standing at the pump, in Cassie's blind spot. She had her head turned away, looking out at the highway.

McWilliams might be looking for me by now. I could have stuck around, done what he'd wanted. I guess I'm not so good taking orders. I thought about walking around the back of the truck, getting in, driving back home. Saying something to her about the price of gas. The weather. Then we could sit down for hamburgers and fries, talk about movies and television shows. Whatever it is people do. Like my parents had done for years. How was work? Fine. How was your work? Fine. Or we could drive off somewhere else, forget about her uncle and Franklin Rudd. Forget about my grandfather, too.

Maybe every choice is a bullet. Doesn't matter which one you choose. All works out the same.

I paid for the gas, slid back into the truck, drove along until we stopped to eat.

+ + +

When we hit Rosston a little later, Cassie opened the Styrofoam box of leftover fries between us. "This Mr. Rudd old?"

"Pretty much, I figure."

"Where's he living?"

"Athens. With some family."

"How'd you find all that out?"

"I talked to a couple people this morning, asked some questions." I wiped the French fry grease on my pants.

"So you just want to talk to him?"

"Just want to ask him some questions."

"And then?"

"What do you mean?"

One of the tires was sounding thin on the pavement, pulling toward the ditch. One of those times you can stop, put a few pounds in if you can find a place with air. Or you can just keep going, hope it holds.

"I mean you ask him some questions and then we're done with him? Maybe we can just go somewhere else. You ever been to Murray Lake? My family has a little cabin near there. Maybe we could go there after you ask him your questions."

"Guess it depends on the answers."

"Oh," she said, looking out the window.

"Besides, I'm not sure what kind of shape he's in."

"What do you mean?"

"Some kind of cancer," I said. "Spent a few months last year in Little Rock. A hospital."

"So he's dying? Jesus," she said.

The headlights coming our way were spreading out as we ended up further from town in the in-between miles. My parents. My grandfather. Her uncle. "Everybody's dying," I said, like it meant something.

"I guess." She closed the box between us. Looked off into the woods and fields running alongside us. "Jesus," she whispered.

I took a breath, watched for the next set of headlights coming our way.

Not sure either one of us ever saw what we were looking for.